ROMAN TALES

Stendhal
Roman Tales

A new translation
by Susan Ashe

With an Introduction and Notes
by Norman Thomas di Giovanni

FRIDAY
BOOKS

The Friday Project
An imprint of HarperCollins Publishers
77–85 Fulham Palace Road
Hammersmith, London W6 8JB
www.thefridayproject.co.uk
www.harpercollins.co.uk

First published by The Friday Project in 2012

Translation of *Roman Tales*
copyright © 2012 by Susan Ashe
Introduction and notes copyright © 2012
by Norman Thomas di Giovanni
This edition © 2012 by Susan Ashe
and Norman Thomas di Giovanni
www.digiovanni.co.uk
www.lucerna.co.uk

Susan Ashe and Norman Thomas di Giovanni
assert the moral right to be identified
as the authors of this work

A catalogue record for this book is available
from the British Library

ISBN 978-0-00-748799-8

Designed and typeset by Marcial Souto,
Barcelona and Buenos Aires

To Francis Spencer

Contents

Introduction

L'Abbesse de Castro, together with the stories 'Vittoria Accoramboni' and 'Les Cenci', first appeared in book form in Paris at the end of 1839. The volume was among the prolific author's last completed works; remarkably, he wrote it in tandem with his long masterpiece *La Chartreuse de Parme*, published that same year. But despite its compelling characters and narrative perfection, *L'Abbesse* remains one of Stendhal's least understood and appreciated novels.

We know a good deal about the origins and history of *The Abbess of Castro* and of Stendhal's other Roman tales. Sometime in March 1833 he acquired from the archives of certain Roman patricians – it is said from the library of the Caetani family – the right to make copies of a number of old and yellowing manuscripts concerning celebrated trials of the sixteenth and seventeenth centuries, which for the most part ended in the torture and brutal execution of the accused. Among these lurid narratives were accounts of popes dispatching cardinals, executions for murder, beheadings, burnings at the stake, and so forth. Most involved high-ranking Church officials and Roman nobility. In 1834 Stendhal records in the margins of one of his own books, '*I have seven* volumes replete with Roman exploits, the telling of which in a translation, without any embellishment, would be sufficiently authentic and typical but probably less entertaining *that* [than] *the actual tales.*' (The italics here and that follow are Stendhal's English, words and phrases of which he habitually interspersed with his French.) On his death the author left another seven volumes of these copied texts. At some point, he singles out the narratives concerning Victoria Accoramboni and the Cenci and sees in some of his material the possibility '*To make . . . a little romanzetto.*' That is, to draft a short novel.

But by 21 December 1834 the author seems to have shifted his position. On this date, writing to the critic Sainte-Beuve, Stendhal says that when he falls on hard times and needs money he will translate some of these manuscripts, and he asks, 'What should the collection be called? *Roman Tales* faithfully translated from accounts written by contemporaries (1400 to 1650). But can the account of a tragedy be called a tale?'

He goes on to tell Sainte-Beuve that these short histories, almost all of them tragic, are written 'in the common speech of the period' and can 'be seen as a useful complement to Italian history' of their day. He characterizes them as composed in 'demijargon', by which he meant semi-dialect. But they aren't – not in the texts I have studied, which are of a simple Italian set down long before the Italian language reached a purified and fixed state.

In fact, Stendhal's translations are more adaptations than the 'faithful' versions he liked to trumpet. As one would expect of an impetuous character like him, he has pared down and uncluttered the Italian texts to make his versions more fluent, more readable. With regard to '*The Bishop of Castro and the Abadessa*', notwithstanding the author's claims that his sources are two manuscripts, one Florentine, the other Roman – claims that he won't let us forget throughout the course of the novel – the *romanzetto* is neither a translation nor an adaptation but an original piece of writing. This is plain to see when the story of Elena and Giulio is compared to other of Stendhal's Roman tales, the so-called faithful translations. The plot, the character of Giulio himself, the sparkling dialogue, the insights into the protagonists' psychology, the melodramatic ending are all pure Stendhalian invention. His only source, the thirty-odd-page manuscript account of the affair, the trial, and the scandal of the Abbess of the Convent of the Visitation and the Bishop of Castro, provided no more than a spur, a point of departure, for one of the author's most perfect creations.

In his lifetime, Stendhal published four of his Roman stories and – as stated – saw but three of them collected in book form. In 1855, some thirteen years after his death, a selection of five of these tales appeared under the name of *Chroniques italiennes* (a title not Stendhal's but that of his cousin Romain Colomb and a title that has persisted down the years). From here on, successive editions of these 'Italian chronicles' have varied in content according to each editor's criteria.

Not all the stories in these collections have their sources in the old copied manuscripts. Recent editions have provided us with supplements and appendixes, often with variants, of a number of unfinished texts. These editions have comprehensive introductions and meticulous notes. Stendhal was a tireless scribbler in the margins of his work, particularly in the Italian manuscripts, and these jottings too are brought to our careful attention. The fascination with this material among Stendhal scholars and fans and the continued overlapping presentation of it is almost claustrophobic.

But what was Stendhal getting at in these Italian tales? What did they represent to him? What was he using them to illustrate? One of the constants throughout his career was his love of Italy, and over and over he reiterates a pet theory – such as the following from the introductory pages of the *Abbess* – that

In sixteenth-century France, a man could show his manhood and true mettle . . . only on the battlefield or in a duel. And as women love bravery and daring, they became the supreme judges of a man's worth. Thus gallantry was born. This led to the successive destruction of all passions, including love . . .

In Italy, a man could distinguish himself as much by the discovery of an old manuscript as by the sword . . . A sixteenth-century woman would love a man who was versed in ancient Greek as much or more than one renowned for his courage in war. Passions rather than gallantry held sway.

A short note to the reader on the first pages of *The Charterhouse of Parma* states that 'the Italians are sincere, honest folk and . . . say what is in their minds; it is only when the mood seizes them that they show any vanity; which then becomes passion . . .' Again, in a preface to his story of the Duchess of Palliano, Stendhal speaks of 'the unfettered passion that appeared in Italy in the sixteenth and seventeenth centuries and that died out in our time owing to the aping of French customs and Parisian fashion'. He tells us he will not in his translation 'make any attempt to adorn the simplicity, the occasionally startling crudeness' of the narrative. He saw that the essence of this passion rested on the fact that it sought its own satisfaction and was not bound up in vanity. Such passionate feeling required deeds, not words. Stendhal warned his readers that very little conversation would be found in his Italian tales. 'This is a handicap to my translation, accustomed as we are in our fiction to long conversations by the characters . . .'

All these claims except one are perfectly illustrated

in his story of the tragic love affair of Giulio Branciforte and Elena de' Compireali. The remark about long conversations, however, is a flat contradiction of what he wrote, the way he wrote it, and of the resulting spell he cast in *The Abbess of Castro*.

Marie-Henri Beyle, best known by his favourite pen name Stendhal, was born in Grenoble on 23 January 1783. His immediate family was pious, royalist, and firmly conservative, whereas from an early age young Beyle came to despise convention, was an atheist, and, as a follower of Napoleon, a fervent advocate of the French Revolution.

The details of his life, the range of his experiences, his tireless travels, are truly extraordinary. He adored women and had countless women friends and lovers, none forgettable, none forgotten, and all his liaisons ultimately unsuccessful; he never married. He understood women and wrote about them in a way that is revolutionary and still unmatched. His female characters Madame de Rênal and Mathilde de la Mole (*The Red and the Black*), Gina Sanseverina and Clelia Conti (*The Charterhouse of Parma*), Vittoria Carafa and Elena de' Campireali (*The Abbess of Castro*), and even Lamiel in the author's last and unfinished eponymous novel, are among the greatest creations in all literature.

Beyle left Grenoble for Paris at the end of 1799, whereupon influential relatives got him a post as a lowly clerk in the Ministry of War. He was only seven-teen when in May 1800 he was allowed to follow Napoleon's army into Italy, where he found a position doing clerical work for the governor of Lombardy. Here he fell in love with Italy, with Italian opera, with Milan, and was enthralled by the city's relaxed atmosphere. Later he was to write, 'were I to follow nothing but my inclination, I should never set foot outside Milan.' By September he was appointed a sub-lieutenant in the dragoons (without knowing how to ride a horse) and aide-de-camp of General Claude Michaud.

Thus began a farcical army career, which he really detested, but that allowed him to witness battles in Austria, Germany, and Russia. In 1812 he saw the torching of the Russian capital and soon after joined in the French army's ill-fated retreat from Moscow.

After the fall of Napoleon Beyle retired to Italy, where he lived the life of a penurious dilettante and began to write. His first books, lives of Haydn, Mozart, and Metastasio, and a history of Italian painting, were largely cribbed compilations – a practice widespread at the time – that he signed with different pen names. It is said that, as a form of protective cover, Beyle used in his life and in his writing up to a hundred different pseudonyms.

There followed a series of travel books on Italy, whose cities and towns he explored and researched assiduously. The chatty volume *Rome, Naples et*

Florence en 1817 was his first success as an author; the French text was reissued in London in 1817, and the next year appeared in an English translation. This was the earliest of his books to bear the pen name Stendhal. In 1822 he published a semi-didactic, semi-autobiographical dissertation on love.

Armance, the first of his novels, appeared in 1827, followed three years later by *The Red and the Black*. In 1830 he entered the civil service and was appointed consul at Civitavecchia. The post he really coveted was at Austrian Trieste, but Stendhal's association with Italian patriots who were plotting for national independence made him a persona non grata with the Austrians, and he was turned down. With little else to do in sleepy Civitavecchia, he began the novel *Lucien Leuwen*, which he left unfinished and which remained unpublished until 1894. From 1836 to 1839 he took sick leave and returned to Paris, where he began a life of Napoleon and completed two more novels, *The Charterhouse of Parma* and *The Abbess of Castro*.

For a while Stendhal supported himself by journalism, writing cultural articles for three or four English reviews. He also kept a diary and undertook a series of autobiographical writings, all unpublished in his lifetime. His fiction, while admired by a small circle of literary figures such as Balzac and Mérimée, did not sell, and the general public found his work incomprehensible and eccentric. The proverbial outsider, he himself predicted that his books would only be discovered and read fifty years after his death. This proved an uncannily accurate assessment.

Beyle died in Paris on 23 March 1842 and was interred in Montmartre cemetery. It is said that three persons attended the funeral.

Susan Ashe's translation, designed for the contemporary reader, concentrates on the narrative drive and drama of each story. This has meant taming a number of the author's excesses. Stendhal, who wrote and dictated with notorious speed, is guilty in descriptive passages of the careless repetition of words and phrases that today we find only clumsy and annoying. Another peccadillo, eliminated in the current version, is his now pointless footnotes that translate for us the value of items in terms of French currency of the 1830s. Also eliminated are footnoted references to obscure works such as Montesquieu's *Politique de Romains dans la religion* or Saint-Simon's *Mémoires de l'abbé Blache*, which it is doubtful any reader today would trouble themselves over. The chief items to have been pruned, however, are the repeated references in *The Abbess of Castro* by which Stendhal sought to convince us that the story is not his but the work of Florentine and Roman antiquarians. These passages are both feeble and unconvincing.

Of course, the above confessions will offend purists. The field of translation is awash with quibbles regarding purity and fidelity. A good translation, however, does not try to duplicate the original but strikes out on its own. Anyone wishing to read Stendhal untouched and unadulterated can do so ungrumblingly in the author's native French.

'Vittoria Accoramboni' was first published, unsigned, in *La Revue des deux mondes*, 1 March 1837. It should be pointed out that Webster's 1612 play *The White Devil* was based on this same story.

'Les Cenci', also unsigned, made its first appearance in *La Revue des deux mondes*, 1 July 1837.

'L'Abbesse de Castro', under the pen name F. de Lagenevais, saw first light in *La Revue de deux mondes*, 1 February and 1 March 1839. When *The Abbess* was published in book form the author's name appeared as Stendhal.

Stendhal's works are currently issued, with more to come, in seven volumes in the Bibliothèque de la Pléiade.

Norman Thomas di Giovanni
Keyhaven, Lymington
Hampshire
January 2012

Acknowledgements

Thanks are due once more to our publisher Scott Pack for his rare ability to take on a project without a moment's hesitation. The editorial world needs fifty more like him. Thanks also to Tom di Giovanni for his clear-sighted dissection of these introductory pages and his succinct suggestions for improving them. And to Liz Cowen for her advice and for her scrupulous copyediting.

THE ABBESS OF CASTRO

I

Sixteenth-century Italian brigands have so often been depicted in melodrama, and so many people have talked about them without knowing anything, that our impression of these outlaws is now utterly false. Broadly speaking, they could be called the opposition to the appalling governments which, in Italy, followed upon the medieval republics. A defunct republic's richest citizen generally became the new tyrant, and, to curry favour with the common people, he would lavish on a town fine paintings and magnificent churches.

Of such were the Polentini clan of Ravenna, the Manfredi of Faenza, the Riario of Imola, the Cani of Verona, the Bentivoglio of Bologna, the Visconti of Milan, and last – the least martial but most hypocritical of all – the Medici of Florence. None of the historians of these small principalities dared mention the countless poisonings and assassinations that the fear gripping these petty tyrants demanded, for all these earnest chroniclers were in their pay. When we realize that each of the tyrants knew intimately each of the republicans who hated him (the Tuscan Grand

Duke Cosimo, for instance, was well acquainted with Strozzi) and that many of these tyrants were themselves assassinated, we can fathom the deep hatred and endless distrust that endowed sixteenth-century Italians with such spirit and courage and their artists with such inspiration.

In sixteenth-century France a man could show his manhood and true mettle – and win admiration for bravery – only on the battlefield or in a duel. And as women love bravery and daring, they became the supreme judges of a man's worth. Thus gallantry was born. This led to the successive destruction of all passions, including love, thereby benefitting that cruel tyrant whom we all obey – vanity. Kings nurtured vanity, and with good reason. Thus the potency of medals and honours.

In Italy a man could distinguish himself as much by the discovery of an old manuscript as by the sword. Look at Petrarch, the idol of his times. A sixteenth-century woman would love a man who was versed in ancient Greek as much or more than one renowned for his courage in war. Passions rather than gallantry held sway. This is why Italy gave birth to a Raphael, a Giorgione, a Titian, and a Correggio, while France produced all the brave commanders of the sixteenth century, each of whom slew numberless numbers of the enemy and yet today are utterly unknown.

Forgive me for speaking the blunt truth. The cruel but necessary acts of revenge committed by medieval petty tyrants reconciled the people to banditry. Brigands were hated when they stole horses, grain, money – in short, all the necessities of life – but in their hearts the people sided with these outlaws. Village maidens favoured above all others the young man who was forced at least once in his life, because of some reckless deed, to flee to the woods and seek refuge among brigands.

Nowadays everyone dreads an encounter with brigands, but, when they are caught and punished, we all sympathize with them. The fact is that shrewd, cynical people, who mock all edicts issued by their masters, revel in reading little poems that glowingly describe the lives of well-known outlaws. What is seen as heroic in these stories thrills the artistic vein that still survives in the lower classes. Moreover, they are so tired of the official praise doled out to certain parties that anything unofficial goes straight to their hearts.

We should understand that in Italy the common people suffer from problems that the tourist wouldn't be aware of even if he lived in the country for a decade. Fifteen years ago, for example, before the government in its wisdom stamped out brigands, it was not unusual to find that some of their exploits punished the crimes of small-town governors. These governors, absolute despots who were never paid more than twenty scudi a month, were naturally at the beck and call of the most important family, which, accordingly, was able to oppress its enemies.

If the brigands weren't always able to punish these petty despots, at least they taunted and defied them, which is no small thing in the eyes of a quick-witted people. A satirical sonnet could make up for all their ills, and they never forgot an insult. This is another of the big differences between the Italian and the Frenchman.

In the sixteenth century, if the governor of a town sentenced to death some poor soul hated by an influential family, brigands would often launch a raid on the prison and try to free the victim. The powerful family, not placing much trust in the eight or nine government soldiers guarding the prison, would at its own expense levy an ad hoc militia. These men, known as *bravi*, would camp near the prison and escort to the place of execution the poor devil whose death had been purchased. A young man from the powerful family would be made captain of these novice soldiers.

Such a situation must surely have made upright men groan. Nowadays we have duels and boredom, and judges do not sell themselves, but sixteenth-century customs were marvellously suited to creating men worthy of the name.

Many historians, still praised in the hack writing of academics, have tried to conceal this state of affairs, which around 1550 was shaping such great individuals. In their day these historians were rewarded for their tactful lies with all the honours that the Medici of Florence, the d'Este of Ferrara, and the viceroys of Naples could bestow. One unfortunate historian, Pietro Giannone, tried to lift a corner of the veil but as he only dared tell part of the truth – and in the local dialect – what he wrote was not understood, which did not prevent him from dying in prison on 7 March 1758 at the age of eighty-two.

If anyone wants to know the history of Italy, the important thing is not to read the widely accepted authors. Nowhere has the value of a lie been better appreciated, nowhere better paid.

Even the earliest histories of Italy, written after the great barbarian wave of the ninth century, mention brigands and speak of them as if they'd existed from time immemorial. When, unfortunately for the general well-being of the people and justice and good government – but fortunately for the arts – the medieval republics were overturned, the most active republicans, who loved freedom more than a good many of their fellow citizens, took refuge in the forests. Naturally, anyone persecuted by the Baglioni, the Malatesta, the Bentivoglio, the Medici, and so forth, loved and respected the enemies of these tyrants. The cruel practices of the petty rulers who succeeded the early usurpers – for instance, the brutality of Cosimo, the first Duke of Florence, who'd assassinated the republicans who had fled to Venice and Paris – sent recruits to the brigands.

If we consider only the period when our heroine

lived – around 1550 – Alfonso Piccolomini, Duke of
Monte Mariano, and Marco Sciarra successfully led
armed bands which, near Albano, defied the pope's
own brave soldiers. The territory of these notorious
chieftains stretched from the Po and the Ravenna
marshes to the forests which then clothed the slopes
of Vesuvius. The Faggiola forest, Sciarra's stamping
ground – five leagues from Rome along the road to
Naples – was made famous by his exploits. Here,
several times during the papacy of Gregory XIII, Sciarra
assembled a band of several thousand soldiers. An
accurate account of this brigand's history would seem
incredible to the present generation, none of whom
could begin to unravel the motives for his deeds. He
was undefeated until 1592. When at last he realized
the desperate straits he was in, he made terms with the
Venetian Republic and, with his most trusted (or
most guilty) soldiers, went into its service. On the
request of the Roman government, Venice, which
had signed a treaty with Sciarra, had him put to
death and sent his brave soldiers to defend the island
of Crete against the Turks. The crafty Venetians
knew that a deadly plague was raging there, and in
few days Sciarra's five hundred men were reduced to
sixty-seven.

The Faggiola forest, whose gigantic trees clothe
an extinct volcano, was the scene of Marco Sciarra's
final exploits. Travellers will tell you that this is the
most magnificent part of the Roman plain and that

its sombre aspect seems made for tragedy. Its dark foliage crowns the summit of Monte Albano.

A volcanic eruption many centuries before the founding of Rome gave birth to this imposing mountain. It emerged from a wide plain which then stretched from the Apennines to the sea. Monte Cavo, which rises from the gloomy shade of the Faggiola wood, is the highest point. The panorama extends from Terracina to Ostia and from Rome to Tivoli. Monte Albano, now decked out in palazzi, comprises Rome's southern horizon, which is so instantly recognizable to travellers.

A Blackfriars monastery on top of Monte Cavo has replaced the temple of Jupiter Feretrius, where the Latin peoples offered sacrifices and strengthened the bonds of a sort of religious federation. In a few hours, shaded by the branches of huge chestnut trees, the traveller will reach the great stones which are the remnants of the temple of Jupiter. But beneath the dark foliage, so welcome in this climate, even the modern traveller, fearing brigands, nervously eyes the forest depths.

On the summit of Monte Cavo, you may light a fire in the temple ruins to prepare a meal. West from this spot, the sea seems but a step or two away although it is really three of four leagues. You can glimpse tiny boats. Even with weak binoculars you can count the passengers on the Naples steamer. In every other direction, the view takes in the magnificent plain which, beyond Palestrina, is bordered in the east by the Apennines and to the north by St Peter's and other great Roman buildings. Since Monte Cavo is not high, the eye can pick out every tiny detail of this superb landscape, which could dispense with any historical association were it not for the fact that each clump of trees, each section of ruined wall on the plain or on the hillside bears witness to a battle, recorded by Livy and famed for its patriotism and courage.

To reach the remnants of the temple of Jupiter Feretrius, whose huge stones now wall the Black-friars' garden, we take the triumphal way trodden by the first kings of Rome. The road is paved with regularly cut slabs. Long stretches have been found in the middle of the Faggiola forest.

Inside the rim of the extinct crater, which is five or six miles round, is the lovely lake of Albano. Here, deeply embedded in the lava rock, stood Alba, the forerunner of Rome, which the Romans destroyed in the days of the early kings. Its ruins are still here. Several centuries later, a quarter of a league from Alba, modern Albano grew up on the flank of the mountain facing the sea. But the town is separated from the lake by a curtain of rocks, so that the one is hidden from the other. Seen from the plain, Albano's white buildings rise out of the dark foliage of the forest, much loved by brigands and by writers, that clads every side of the volcanic mountain.

Now a town of five or six thousand inhabitants, Albano had only three thousand in 1540, when the powerful Campireali family, whose ill-fated tale we are about to tell, was among the leading ranks of the nobility.

This story has been translated from two long manuscripts, one Roman, the other Florentine. At my peril I have ventured to reproduce their style, which is akin to that of our old legends. The more refined style of the present age would, I think, be out of keeping with the authors' observations and the events they describe. They were writing in about 1598. For them and for myself, I beg the reader's indulgence.

II

After recording numerous tragic stories, says the author of the Florentine manuscript, he will end with the one he found the most painful. This is the tale of the notorious Elena de' Campireali, Abbess of the Convent of the Visitation in Castro, whose trial and death gave Roman and Neapolitan society so much food for gossip.

In 1555, while brigands roamed the outskirts of Rome, magistrates were in the pay of powerful families. In the year 1572, when the abbess's trial took place, Pope Gregory XIII came to the throne of St Peter. This holy pontiff possessed all the apostolic virtues but his civic rule could be accused of certain weaknesses. He neither chose honest judges nor controlled the brigands; he fretted over crimes but felt unable to punish them. He believed that in inflicting the death penalty he was taking on a fearful responsibility.

As a consequence, the roads to the eternal city were infested by an endless host of brigands. To travel safely one had to befriend the outlaws. The Faggiola forest, which straddles the road from Albano to

Naples, had for many years been the headquarters of a force hostile to His Holiness, and often Rome had to make treaties, as if with a foreign power, with Marco Sciarra, one of the kings of the forest. The brigands' strength lay in the fact that they were liked by their peasant neighbours.

Elena de' Campireali was born in 1542 in the lovely town of Albano, very near the brigands' stamping ground. Her father was the area's richest man, and as such he had married Vittoria Carafa, who owned large estates in the Kingdom of Naples. Vittoria was a model of prudence and good sense. In spite of her intelligence, however, she could not stem the downfall of her family. Unusually, the calamities which are the sad subject of this tale cannot be blamed on any of its characters. Elena's great beauty and tender heart, which left her vulnerable, excuse Giulio Branciforte, her lover. Equally, because of his complete lack of common sense, the Bishop of Castro, Monsignor Cittadini is to a certain extent exonerated. He owed his swift advance in ecclesiastical honours to his honest conduct and above all to the noblest bearing and most handsome face that anyone could hope to encounter. It has been said that to see him was to love him.

A holy monk of the Monastery of Monte Cavo, who was frequently found in his cell levitating several feet off the ground when only divine grace could have kept him in this extraordinary position, had told Signor de' Campireali that his family would die with him and that he would have but two children, both of whom would meet violent deaths. It was owing to this prophecy that Signor de' Campireali could not marry in his own region but went to seek his fortune in Naples, where he had the luck to find great wealth and a wife capable by her own wits of changing his ill-starred destiny, if such a thing were possible. Signor de' Campireali was an honest man and he made many charitable donations, but, lacking in cleverness, he withdrew from Rome and ended by spending almost the whole year in his palazzo in Albano. He devoted himself to farming his lands, which lay on the rich plain between the town and the sea. Thanks to his wife, he gave his son Fabio, a young man proud of his birth, the best possible education. He did the same for his daughter Elena, who was a miracle of beauty, as can still be seen by her portrait in the Farnese collection.

In this picture, Elena's face is oval-shaped, with a high forehead and dark blonde hair. She has a glint in her large, deeply expressive eyes, and her chestnut brows form perfect arcs. Her lips are fine, and her mouth looks as if it were drawn by Correggio. Seen among the portraits hanging in the Farnese, she has the air of a queen. A cheerful look and regal bearing are not often found together.

Elena spent eight whole years as a boarder in the Convent of the Visitation in the town of Castro, which no longer exists but where in those days the daughters of most Roman princes were sent. She then came home, but on leaving the convent she made it the gift of a magnificent chalice. As soon as she returned to Albano, her father, by means of a large retaining fee, had the renowned poet Cechino, then a very old man, brought from Rome. He embellished Elena's memory with the most beautiful verses by the divine Vergil, Petrarch, Ariosto, and Dante.

Elena seems to have known Latin. The poems she learned spoke of love, the passionate love that takes sustenance from great sacrifices, lives wrapped in mystery, and always goes hand in hand with terrible tragedy.

Such was the love Giulio Branciforte inspired in Elena, then scarcely seventeen years old. A neighbour of hers, he lived in a humble house in the mountains. A quarter of a league from the town, it stood among the ruins of Alba on the edge of the hundred-and-fifty-foot precipice carpeted with greenery that circled the lake.

Giulio had little in his favour but a cheerful spirit and the carefree way in which he bore his poverty. His face was expressive without being handsome. He was known to have fought bravely under the command of Prince Colonna and among his *bravi* in two or three dangerous enterprises. In spite of his poverty, in spite of a lack of good looks, Giulio Branciforte – according to the young girls of Albano – already possessed the heart of the one he would have been most flattered to win. Well received everywhere, he had only had trifling love affairs until Elena returned from the convent.

Shortly afterwards, Cechino moved from Rome to the Palazzo Campireali to teach literature to the young girl. Giulio, who knew the great poet, wrote him a poem in Latin on how fortunate he was in his old age to see such beautiful eyes fixed on his and to behold a soul so pure.

The jealousy and spite of the young girls Giulio had courted before Elena's return soon made it useless for him to try to hide his growing passion, and so this love between a young man of twenty-two and a girl of seventeen took a path that cannot be called cautious. Not three months went by before Signor de' Campireali noticed that Giulio Branciforte passed too often beneath the windows of his palazzo.

Outspokenness and bluntness, which always follow the freedom republics allow and the free rein given to passions as yet unsuppressed by the manners of a monarchy, could be seen in Campireali's first step. On the very day he was upset by young Branciforte's too frequent appearances he spoke to him.

'How dare you keep traipsing past my house and gazing up impertinently at my daughter's window', he said, 'when you barely have a decent garment to cover yourself? If I were not afraid my neighbours would misconstrue it, I'd give you a couple of gold coins and send you to Rome to buy a better tunic. At least my eyes and my daughter's would be less affronted by the sight of your rags.'

Elena's father was exaggerating. Young Branciforte's clothes were not rags but were made of homespun. Although clean and cared for, they were somewhat threadbare. Giulio was so deeply wounded by Campireali's insults that he never again passed the house in daylight.

Two arches – remnants of an ancient aqueduct – served as the main walls of the house built and left to Giulio by his father. The place was only five or six hundred yards from Albano. To descend from here to the new town, Giulio had to pass the Palazzo Campireali. Elena soon noted the absence of this strange man who had, so his friends claimed, given up all other ties to devote himself wholly to the happiness he seemed to find in gazing at her.

One summer evening towards midnight Elena was at her open window enjoying the air which reaches Albano from the sea three leagues away. The night was dark, the silence deep. You could have heard a leaf drop. Leaning on her windowsill, Elena was perhaps thinking of Giulio, when an object like the silent wing of a night bird brushed against her window.

She drew back in alarm. The window was on the second storey, more than fifty feet above the ground. All at once, the girl thought she saw a posy moving back and forth in the deep silence. Her heart beat wildly. The posy seemed to be tied to the end of two or three long canes attached to each other. The pliancy of the rods and the breeze made it difficult for Giulio to keep his bouquet in front of the window where he guessed Elena might be. The night was so dark that from the road nothing could be seen at such a height.

Standing at her window, Elena was deeply troubled. Would taking the posy mean giving her consent? She felt none of the emotions her situation would have aroused in a well-brought-up young girl of today. Her father and brother Fabio were in the house. Elena's first thought was that the slightest sound would be followed by a weapon fired at Giulio. She pitied the young man for the risk he was taking. Her next thought was that although she hardly knew him he was nevertheless the person whom, after her family, she loved best in the world. After several seconds' hesitation, she took the posy and, touching the flowers in the inky blackness, she felt a piece of paper tied to the stem of one bloom. She ran to the great staircase to read the note by the glimmer of the lamp glowing before a portrait of the Madonna.

'Rash boy,' she said, when the first lines made her blush with pleasure. 'If anyone sees me I'm lost, and my family will persecute this poor young man for ever.'

She returned to her room and lit a lamp. It was a

thrilling moment for Giulio, who, ashamed of what he was doing and as if to hide even in the dark, was clinging to the huge trunk of one of the curiously shaped green oaks which still grow in front of the Palazzo Campireali.

In the letter, Giulio described straightforwardly the mortifying reprimand he'd had from Elena's father.

I am poor, it's true, and it would be hard for you to understand just how poor. I have only my house, which you may have noticed under the ruined aqueduct of Alba. There's a garden round it, which I cultivate myself and whose plants nourish me. I also have a vineyard that brings me thirty scudi a year. I really don't know why I love you. Obviously I can't invite you to share my poverty. But at the same time, if you don't care for me at all my life is worth nothing. It's useless to say that I would give it a thousand times for you. Before you came back from the convent, my life was not miserable. On the contrary, it was filled with the most exciting plans. Now this glimpse of happiness has made me wretched. No one else would have dared utter the insults your father lashed me with. My dagger would have given me instant justice. My courage and my dagger made me the equal of anyone in the world. I lacked nothing. Now everything has changed. I know fear. Perhaps I go on too long. Perhaps you despise me. If, however, you have some pity for me in spite of the humble clothes I wear, every evening when midnight sounds at the Capuchin monastery on the top of the hill you will see that I am hiding under the great oak opposite the balcony I watch endlessly because I believe it to be your bedroom window. If you do not despise me as your father does, throw me one of the flowers from the posy, but take care it does not catch on the corner of the balcony below.

Elena read the letter several times, her eyes slowly filling with tears. She was moved by the beautiful bouquet, which was tied with a strong silken thread. She tried to pluck out a flower but did not succeed. Suddenly she was filled with remorse. To Roman girls, plucking a flower from a posy given as a love token or destroying it in any way risks killing off that love. Fearing Giulio's impatience, she dashed to the window. Once there, she thought she could be seen too easily. The lamp filled the room with light. Elena did not know what signal she could allow herself. There seemed nothing that would not say too much.

Timid, she hurried back into her room. But time passed. Then a thought filled her with anxiety. Giulio would think that she too despised him for his poverty. A small piece of precious marble lay on a table. Knotting it in her handkerchief, she threw it to the foot of the oak opposite her window. Then she signed to him to go away. She heard Giulio obey. As he left he did not trouble to conceal the sound of his footsteps. When he reached the top of the ring of rocks that separates the lake from Albano, she heard him break into a love song. Less timid now, she waved to him, then went back to reread her letter.

The next day and the following days there were similar letters and assignations. But as nothing goes unnoticed in an Italian village, and Elena's family was by far the richest in the region, Signor de' Campireali was informed that every evening after midnight a light could be seen in his daughter's room. And, stranger still, the window was open and Elena stood there as if she had no fear of irksome busybodies. Signor de' Campireali got out his arquebus and his son's. That evening, as a quarter to midnight struck, he called Fabio, and, making as little noise as possible, the two slipped out onto a large stone balcony immediately below Elena's window. The thick columns of the stone balustrade protected them below the waist from gunshots that might be fired on them from without. Midnight struck; father and son could clearly hear rustling sounds from the trees that bordered the road opposite the palazzo, but to their surprise no light appeared in Elena's window.

Falling in love had changed this girl from a simple carefree child. She knew that the slightest reckless action could spell death to her lover. Should someone as important as her father kill a poor man like Giulio Branciforte, he would have to disappear to Naples for three months. Meanwhile his Roman friends would make arrangements, and all would be settled by the gift of a silver lamp worth several hundred scudi to the altar of whichever Madonna was then in fashion.

That morning, at breakfast, Elena noted from her

father's expression that he was extremely angry, and, by the way he watched her when he thought she was not looking, she realized she was the source of his anger. Quickly she sprinkled a layer of dust on the stocks of the five magnificent arquebuses her father kept hanging by his bed. She also scattered a thin coat of dust over his daggers and swords. All day in a state of excitement she ran up and down the house. She kept going to the windows, ready to wave Giulio away if she caught sight of him. But she needn't have worried. After her father's humiliating reprimand Giulio never came to Albano by day except, out of duty, to Sunday Mass. Elena's mother, who adored her and refused her nothing, went out with her three times that day. But it was no use. Elena saw no sign of Giulio. She was desperate.

What can she have felt when that evening, going to inspect her father's weapons, she saw that two arquebuses had been loaded and that most of the daggers and swords had been handled. She was only distracted from her deathly anguish by the extreme care she took to seem to suspect nothing. When she retired to bed at ten o'clock that night she locked the door of her room, which opened into her mother's antechamber. She stayed close to the window, lying on the floor in such a way that she couldn't be seen from outside. We can well imagine the anxiety with which she heard each hour strike. She no longer felt that her impetuous attachment to Giulio might in his eyes make her less worthy of love. That single day advanced the young man's courtship further than six months of constancy and avowals of love.

'What's the use of lying?' Elena asked herself. 'Do I not love him with all my soul?'

At half-past eleven she clearly saw her father and brother stationing themselves for an ambush on the balcony below her window. Two minutes after midnight sounded at the Capuchin monastery, she also heard her lover's footsteps halting beneath the large oak. She noticed with relief that her father and brother seemed to have heard nothing. Only love's heedfulness could make out such a soft rustle.

'They're going to kill me,' she thought, 'but they must not find tonights's letter. They will hunt down poor Giulio for ever.' She made the sign of the cross and, with one hand gripping the iron railing of her window, she leaned out as far as possible. Before a quarter of a minute had passed, the posy, attached as usual to the long rod, brushed against her arm. She reached for the bouquet but in snatching the rod she accidentally knocked it against the balcony below. Instantly, two shots rang out followed by complete silence. Fabio, thinking in the dark that what had grazed the balcony might be a rope by which Giulio was climbing down from his sister's room, had fired at her balcony. The next day, she found the mark of the ball, which had smashed against the iron railing. Signor de' Campireali had fired into the road below, as Giulio had made a slight sound while trying to prevent the rod from falling.

Hearing noises overhead, Giulio had guessed what was to follow and had taken refuge under the overhang of the balcony.

Fabio quickly reloaded his arquebus and, against his father's orders, ran into the garden, opened a little door which led to the street, and stealthily scrutinized the people who were strolling under the palazzo balcony. At that point, Giulio, who was not alone that evening, clung to a tree twenty paces from Fabio. Elena, leaning against the parapet of her balcony and trembling for her lover, launched into a loud conversation with her brother, asking if he had killed the thieves.

'Don't think you can fool me with your tricks, you slut,' he cried out from the road, where he was prowling about. 'Start weeping, as I'm going to kill the scoundrel who dares approach your window.'

He had hardly spoken when Elena heard her mother knocking on her bedroom door. The girl rushed to open it, saying she had no idea how the door came to be locked.

'Don't play the fool with me, my love,' said her mother. 'Your father is furious and may well kill you. Come and get into my bed with me and if you have a letter let me have it. I'll hide it.'

'Here's the bunch of flowers,' Elena told her. 'The letter is hidden inside it.'

No sooner were mother and daughter in bed when Signor de' Campireali burst into his wife's room. He was on the way back from his oratory, where he had turned everything upside-down. It struck Elena that her father was as pale as a ghost and that he moved like a man who had learned his part perfectly. 'I'm doomed,' the girl told herself.

Approaching his wife's bed on his way to his daughter's room, shaking with fury but pretending to be completely calm, he said, 'We rejoice in our children but we should weep tears of blood when those children are girls. Good God, is it possible their silliness can wipe out the honour of a man who for sixty years has not had the least taint upon him?'

With these words, he went to his daughter's room.

'He's bound to find the letters,' said Elena to her mother. 'They are under the pedestal of the crucifix by the window.'

At once her mother leapt from the bed and ran after her husband. Crying out the worst things she could think of, she sent him into a rage. Blinded by fury, the old man tore his daughter's room apart, but her mother was able to remove the letters without his seeing. An hour later, when Signor de' Campireali had gone back to his own room, the house grew quiet again.

'Here are your letters,' Elena's mother said. 'I don't want to read them. See what they nearly caused us. If I were you I'd burn them. Goodnight. Give me a kiss.'

Elena returned to her room in floods of tears. After what her mother had said, it seemed to the girl that she no longer cared for Giulio. She was about to burn the letters, but she could not stop herself rereading them first. So often and so closely did she study them that the sun was already high in the sky when at last she decided to follow her mother's sensible advice.

The next day, a Sunday, Elena set off with her mother to the parish church. Luckily, her father did not accompany them. The first person she saw in the church was Giulio Branciforte. One look sufficed to see that he was unhurt. Her happiness knew no bounds, and the night's events fled from her memory. She had prepared five or six little notes, jotted on scraps of dirty old paper picked up from the floor of the church. They all had the same message. 'They know everything except his name. Let him not be seen in the road again. We will come here often.'

Elena dropped one of these scraps. A glance told Giulio, who picked it up and left. On her way home an hour later, another scrap of paper caught her attention on the steps of the palazzo. It looked exactly like the one she had used that morning. She took it without her mother seeing and read it. 'In three days he'll be back from Rome. At about ten o'clock on market days amidst the hubbub someone will start to sing.'

This journey to Rome seemed strange to Elena. 'Is he afraid of my brother's gun?' she wondered. Love forgives all except voluntary absence, which is the worst of tortures. Instead of going by in sweet reverie, counting the reasons for loving a lover, life is beset with cruel suspicions. 'But am I really to believe he no longer loves me?' Elena wondered over the three long days of Branciforte's absence. Her sorrow gave way to great joy when on the third day she saw him at midday coming along the road past her father's palazzo. Giulio's clothes were new, almost sumptuous. Never had his noble bearing and the brave carefree candour of his face appeared to greater advantage. Before now everyone in Albano had talked about Giulio's poverty. It was the young men in particular who spoke of it most often, while the women, especially the girls, never stopped praising his handsome face.

Giulio spent the whole day strolling about the town. He seemed to be making up for the months of solitude his poverty had condemned him to. As befits a man in love, he was well armed beneath his new tunic. Besides his dirk and dagger, he wore a *giacca*, a mail waistcoat, which was uncomfortable but which cured Italian hearts of a woeful sickness to whose sharp attacks a man was ceaselessly prone in those days. This was the fear of being killed at every bend in the road by one of his enemies.

That day Giulio was hoping to catch a glimpse of Elena and, furthermore, he did not relish the idea of being alone in his isolated house. This is why.

Ranuccio, one his father's former soldiers, who

had served with him in ten campaigns in various condottieri regiments – most recently under Marco Sciarra – had followed his captain until his wounds forced him to retire. Captain Branciforte had reasons for not living in Rome. There he ran the risk of meeting the sons of men he had killed. Even in Albano he took care to steer clear of the legal authorities. Rather than buy or rent a house in town, he chose to build one in a spot where he could see anyone who approached. He found an ideal site in the ruins of Alba, where, concealed from surprise callers, he could take refuge in the forest, the domain of his old friend and leader, Prince Fabrizio Colonna.

Captain Branciforte did not much care about his son's future. When he retired from service at only fifty, but riddled with wounds, he calculated he could live for another ten years, spending each year a tenth of what he had earned in the looting of towns and villages at which he'd had the honour to partake.

He purchased for his son a vineyard that brought in thirty scudi. This was in response to a bad joke by one of Albano's leading citizens, who had once told him when they were arguing over the interests and the honour of the town that in fact it was the business of a rich landowner like Branciforte to give advice to the elders of Albano. The captain bought the vineyard and announced that he would buy many more when, coming across the wag in a lonely place, he shot him dead.

After eight years of this kind of life, the captain died. His aide-de-camp Ranuccio adored Giulio but, growing tired of idleness, the older man returned to Prince Colonna's service. He often came to visit 'his son Giulio', as he called him, and on the eve of a dangerous assault on the prince's castle of La Petrella, Ranuccio had taken Giulio to fight alongside him.

Noting the boy's prowess, the old soldier said, 'You must be a great simpleton to live near Albano as the lowest and poorest inhabitant of the place when, with your father's name and what I could do for you, you could be one of our leading soldiers of fortune and make yourself a pile of money.'

Giulio was tormented by these his words. He'd learned some Latin from a priest, but as his father had always scoffed at everything the priest said, apart from Latin Giulio had received no education. Despised for his poverty, isolated in his lonely house, he had nevertheless developed a certain degree of good sense whose boldness would have astonished learned men. For instance, before he fell in love with Elena, and without knowing why, he adored fighting but loathed looting and pillage, which, in his father and Ranuccio's eyes, was akin to the short farce that follows the high tragedy. Since Giulio had fallen in love with Elena, the good sense he had acquired through his lonely ponderings tormented him. This soul, once so carefree but now full of passion and misery, dared confide in no one. What would Signor de' Campireali say if he knew Giulio to be a soldier of fortune? Any accusation he could now level against Giulio would be justifiable.

Giulio had always relied on soldiering as a sure means of earning his way when he'd spent what he could get for the gold chains and other trinkets he'd discovered in his father's strongbox. If, poor as he was, Giulio had no scruples about carrying off the daughter of the wealthy Signor de' Campireali, it was because in those days fathers disposed of their possessions as they thought fit, and Signor de' Campireali might well leave his daughter a mere thousand scudi. Giulio was preoccupied with a different problem. First, where would he settle with young Elena once he had carried her off and married her? Second, what would they live on?

After Signor de' Campireali's cutting insult, which so wounded Giulio, he spent two days in a wild state of fury and despair. He had nearly decided to kill the insolent old man and spent night after night in tears, until at last he determined to consult Ranuccio, his only friend in the whole world. But would his friend understand?

Scouring the Faggiola forest in vain, Giulio finally found the old soldier on the Naples road beyond Velletri, where Ranuccio was setting up an ambush. He was lying in wait with a considerable force for Ruiz d'Avalos, the Spanish general, who was on his way to Rome by an inland route, forgetful that just before, in a large gathering, he had spoken scornfully of Prince Colonna's soldiers of fortune. His chaplain reminded the general in no uncertain terms of this little matter. Ruiz d'Avalos decided to arm a ship and proceed to Rome by sea.

As soon as Captain Ranuccio heard Giulio's tale, he said, 'Give me an exact description of this Signor de' Campireali before his rashness costs the life of some worthy citizen of Albano. As soon as we've finished our business here, whatever the outcome, you'll go to Rome and make yourself conspicuous in all the inns and public places. You must not be suspected because of your love for the girl.'

After struggling to calm his father's old friend, Giulio was forced to get angry with him. 'Do you think I'm asking for your sword?' he said. 'I assure you, I have a sword of my own. It's your advice I'm asking for.'

As always, Ranuccio concluded with these words. 'You are young; you've never been wounded. It was a public insult. A man whose honour has been besmirched is despised even by women.'

Giulio told him he wanted to give more thought to what his heart desired. Despite Ranuccio's insistence that he take part in the ambush on the Spanish general's escort, where, he said, there was honour to be won, not to mention doubloons, Giulio returned to his little house. It was there that, on the eve of the day Signor de' Campireali fired on him with his arquebus, Giulio had received Ranuccio and his corporal on their return from Velletri. Ranuccio forced open the little strongbox in which Captain Branciforte used to keep the gold chains and other jewels which he thought it unwise to sell immediately after a raid. Ranuccio found two scudi.

'I advise you to become a monk,' he said to Giulio. 'You have all the qualifications. Love of poverty – here's the proof. And humility. You let yourself be vilified in the middle of the street in full view of everyone by a wealthy citizen of Albano. All you lack is hypocrisy and greed.'

Ranuccio insisted on putting fifty doubloons into the strongbox. 'I give you my word,' he said to Giulio, 'that if in a month's time Signor de' Campireali is not buried with all the honour due his nobility and wealth, my corporal here will come with thirty men and raze your house and burn your miserable furniture. Captain Branciforte's son must not on the excuse of love cut a sorry figure in this world.'

That evening, when Signor de' Campireali and his son fired twice, Ranuccio and his corporal had taken up positions under the stone balcony. Giulio had with difficulty restrained them from killing Fabio or abducting him when he rashly came into the garden. To calm Ranuccio, Giulio reasoned that a young man like Fabio might make something useful of himself, while a guilty old sinner like his father was no good for anything but to be buried.

The day after this exploit Ranuccio hid deep in the forest, and Giulio left for Rome. His pleasure in buying fine clothes with Ranuccio's doubloons was cruelly offset by a very unusual idea for those days and one which led to the success he ultimately achieved. 'Elena must know me for who I am,' he thought. Any other man of his day would simply have revelled in the game of love and carried Elena off, not caring what she might have thought of him or what became of her six months later.

On the afternoon that Giulio displayed the fine clothes he'd bought in Rome, he discovered from his friend old Scotti that Fabio had left town on horseback for a property of his father's down on the plain. Giulio later saw Signor de' Campireali, accompanied by two priests, setting off along the magnificent avenue of green oaks that crowns the rim of the crater in which the lake of Albano lies. Ten minutes later an old woman came marching into the Palazzo Campireali, pretending to be selling fruit.

The first person she met was Elena's maid and confidante Marietta. The girl blushed to the roots of her hair when she was presented with a beautiful bouquet. The letter hidden in it was unusually long. Giulio recounted what had happened to him since the night of the gunshots. But, owing to his unusual modesty, he did not dare admit what any other young man of his time would have been proud to reveal – that he was the son of a captain renowned for his exploits and that he himself had already shown his courage in more than one battle. Giulio could imagine what old Campireali would say about this. Sixteenth-century girls, in sympathy with republican ideas, admired a man much more for what he had made of himself than for the fortune amassed by his forebears or for their famous exploits. That is, girls from the common people thought this way. Daughters of the wealthy or noble classes were afraid of bandits, and, quite naturally, held nobility and wealth in great esteem.

Giulio finished his letter with these words:

I do not know if the fashionable clothes I bought in Rome will banish from your memory the cruel affront someone close to you made about my repulsive appearance. I could have taken revenge; I should have. My honour demanded it. I have not done it because of the tears my revenge would have cost those eyes I adore. This may prove to you, if by chance you still doubt it, that a man can be poor but still have noble sentiments. I have something to confess. I would have no difficulty telling this to any other woman but somehow I tremble at the thought of revealing it to you. It could in an instant destroy the love you have for me, and no protestation on your part would satisfy me. I want to read in your eyes the effect this admission will have. One of these days, at nightfall, I will visit you in the garden behind the palazzo. That day, Fabio and your father will be away. When I'm sure that they will not be able to deprive us of an hour or so of conversation, a man will appear beneath your windows and show the local children a tame fox. Later, when the Ave Maria sounds, you'll hear a gunshot in the distance. At that moment, go to your garden wall and, if you are not alone, sing. If you hear nothing, your slave will appear trembling at your feet and will tell you things that may horrify you. While waiting for this terrible day, I will risk giving you no more midnight posies, but at about two in the morning I will pass by singing, and perhaps from your balcony you'll drop a flower picked from your garden. This may be the last signs of affection you will show your unhappy Giulio.

Three days later, Elena's father and brother rode off to the lands they owned by the sea. They left just before sunset, intending to return at around two in the morning. But as they were about to start back not only their two horses but all the horses on the farm disappeared. Outraged by this daring theft, they searched for their animals, which were not found until the following day. They were grazing in a forest of tall trees beside the sea. The two Campireali men had to return to Albano in an oxcart.

Darkness that evening found Giulio at Elena's feet, and the poor girl glad of the gathering dusk. For the first time she was face to face with the man she loved but to whom she had never spoken.

She uttered a word or two, which restored his courage. Giulio was paler and more shaken than she.

'It's hard for me to speak,' he said. Several blissful moments passed while they looked at each other without a word. Giulio took Elena's hand. She gazed at him closely.

He knew his friends, young Roman rakes, would have advised him to make advances, but the idea horrified him. Yet at the same time he knew that ecstatic state which only love can bring. Time passed swiftly. The Campireali men neared the palace. Honest soul that he was, Giulio realized that he would not find lasting happiness unless he made the terrible admission which would have seemed utter stupidity to his Roman friends.

At last, he said, 'I spoke to you of a confession which perhaps I should not make.' Growing pale, he added, 'Perhaps your feelings for me, on which my life depends, will vanish. You think I'm poor, but that's not the worst of it. I'm an outlaw and the son of an outlaw.'

At his words, rich man's daughter that she was and with all the prejudices of her class, Elena felt she would faint.

'How terrible that would be for poor Giulio,' she thought. 'He will think I despise him.' Leaning against him, she sank into his arms as if in a swoon.

After this night many assignations followed. The danger she was running took away Elena's remorse. Sometimes the dangers were extreme, but they only enflamed these two hearts for whom all feelings arising from their love were joyful. Frequently on the point of surprising the young pair, Fabio and his father were furious at finding themselves defied. Town gossip said Giulio was Elena's lover, yet father and son could detect nothing. Fabio suggested that he be allowed to kill Giulio.

'While he lives, my sister's life is in peril. At any moment honour may force us to drench our hands in the blood of the obstinate girl. She has become so bold she no longer denies her love. You see how she answers our accusations with gloomy silence. Very well, this silence is Giulio Branciforte's death sentence.'

'Remember what his father was,' replied old Campireali. 'We could easily go to Rome for six months, during which time this Branciforte would disappear. But there's the question of his father, who, despite his villainy, was a good and generous man – generous enough to enrich many of his soldiers while he himself stayed poor. Who knows whether he hasn't still got friends either in the Duke of Monte Mariano's company or in Prince Colonna's, which often lies a couple of miles away in the Faggiola forest? In which case we'd be slaughtered without mercy – you, me, and perhaps your poor mother too.'

Several such conversations took place between father and son and were only in part kept from Vittoria Carafa, sending her into despair. In the end, the two men concluded that honour demanded they silence the rumours circulating round Albano. As it was unwise to have Branciforte removed, though he seemed to grow bolder every day and, what was more, now dressed in fine clothes to push his advantage, sometimes even speaking in public either to Fabio or to Signor de' Campireali, they would have to undertake one or perhaps both of the following courses. Either the whole family would go back to live in Rome or Elena must return to the Convent of the Visitation in Castro, where she would remain until they found her a suitable match.

Elena had never confessed her love to her mother. Mother and daughter cared dearly for each other and were always together, yet not a word was uttered on the subject that was of almost equal importance to them both. The matter was only broached when the mother told her daughter that the whole household might be returning to Rome and Elena to Castro for a number of years.

It was rash of Vittoria Carafa to have spoken, and her affection for her daughter was no excuse. Elena, head over heels in love, wanted to prove to her lover that she was not ashamed of his poverty and that her confidence in his honour was boundless.

Unbelievable though it may seem, after so many bold assignations in the garden and once in her own room, Elena was chaste. Steadfast in her virtue, she suggested to her lover that she should leave the palazzo through the garden after midnight and spend the rest of the night in Giulio's little house.

They disguised themselves as Franciscan friars. Tall and slender, Elena looked like a novice of eighteen or twenty. The incredible fact – which confirms the finger of God – is that on the narrow path hewn in the rock that hugs the wall of the Capuchin friary, Giulio and his mistress met Signor de' Campireali and Fabio, who, followed by four well-armed servants and preceded by a page carrying a lighted brand, were returning from Castel Gandolfo, a nearby lake-side town. To allow the lovers to pass, the Campireali men and their servants drew aside to right and left of the eight-foot-wide path. How much better it might have turned out for Elena had she been recognized there and then. She would have been shot dead by her father or brother, and her suffering would have lasted but an instant. But heaven ordained other-wise.

Another strange event occurred during the course of this unexpected encounter. Observing that the elder monk failed to greet either him or his father while passing so close, Fabio cried out, 'What proud rascal of a monk have we here? God knows what he's up to outside the monastery, he and his companion, at this late hour! I have a mind to pull off their hoods and see what they look like.'

At these words, Giulio clutched the dagger under his habit and stepped in front of Elena. He was less than a foot from Fabio, but heaven decreed other-wise and by a miracle calmed the fury of the two young men, who would soon meet each other just as close. At Elena de' Campireali's subsequent trial, this nocturnal excursion was cited as proof of her depravity. It was, however, the madness of a young girl aflame with love but whose heart was pure.

III

The Orsini, perennial rivals of the Colonna and pre-eminent in the villages around Rome, had managed to get the government courts to sentence to death a certain Baldassare Bandini, a rich farmer. Though most of the long list of misdeeds he was accused of would today be criminal offences, in 1559 they were usually regarded in a less severe light. Bandini was held six leagues from Albano in one of the Orsini castles in the mountains near Valmontone.

The chief of the Roman secret police, accompanied by a hundred and fifty of his men, travelled the highroad by night to fetch Bandini and take him to the Tordinona prison, in Rome. Bandini had appealed to Rome against his sentence. As he hailed from La Petrella, the Colonna stronghold, Bandini's wife publicly confronted Fabrizio Colonna.

'Are you going to let one of your faithful servants die?' she demanded.

'It is not God's will that I should in any way fail in the respect I owe the decisions of the courts of my lord the pope,' Colonna replied.

At once his soldiers and all his followers were

ordered to meet near Valmontone, a small town built on a rocky outcrop whose ramparts were formed by an almost vertical precipice sixty to eighty feet high. It was in this town, belonging to the pope, that the Orsini partisans and government secret police had managed to capture Bandini. Among these partisans were Signor de' Campireali and his son Fabio, who were distantly related to the Orsini. Giulio Branciforte and his father, however, had always been of the Colonna faction.

In circumstances where Prince Colonna felt unable to act openly he resorted to a simple ruse. Most of the rich Roman farmers, then as now, belonged to one or other group of penitents. The penitents always appeared in public with their heads covered by a hood that hid their faces and had holes for the eyes. When the Colonna forces did not want it known that they were involved in an exploit, they persuaded their adherents to join them wearing the penitent's costume.

In due course, it transpired that the removal of Bandini, which had been the talk of the town for a fortnight, would take place on a Sunday. That day, at two o'clock in the morning, the governor of Valmontone had the tocsin rung in all the Faggiola forest villages. A large number of peasants obeyed the summons.

As each little group of armed peasants left their village and disappeared into the forest, their number was halved. Colonna's partisans were making for the meeting place set up by Fabrizio. Their leaders seemed convinced there would be no fighting that day, and the men had been ordered to spread this rumour. Prince Fabrizio crossed the forest with a picked band of supporters mounted on half-broken colts from his stud farm. He made a cursory inspection of his various detachments of peasants but he did not speak to them. A single word might have given all away.

The prince, a tall, spare man of unusual strength and agility, was barely forty-five, but his hair and moustache were a striking white. This incongruous feature made him recognizable in places where he would have preferred to remain incognito. As soon as the peasants saw him they cried out, *'Evviva Colonna!'*, and pulled on their hoods. The prince himself wore his hood hanging round his neck so that he could slip it on the moment the enemy was sighted.

They did not have to wait long. The sun was rising as nearly a thousand men of the Orsini faction entered the forest three hundred yards from Fabrizio Colonna's force, who threw themselves to the ground. After the Orsini advance guard passed, the prince mustered his men. He decided to attack Bandini's escort a quarter of an hour after they entered the woods. Here the forest is strewn with boulders fifteen or twenty feet tall. These are lumps of lava, some old, some newer, which the chestnut canopy covers completely, almost cutting out the daylight. As these rockfalls, eroded by the weather, make the ground very rough, to spare the highroad from endless ups and downs the lava has been dug away and in places the road is three or four feet lower than the forest floor.

Around Fabrizio's planned battle site was a grassy clearing crossed at one end by the main road. Thereafter the road re-entered the forest, which here was thick with brambles and thorn bushes, making the undergrowth all but impenetrable. Fabrizio placed his peasants a hundred yards into the forest on either side of the road. At a signal from him, each man drew on his hood and positioned himself behind a tree with his arquebus at the ready. The prince's soldiers hid behind the trees nearest the road. The peasants had express orders not to fire until the soldiers fired, and the soldiers were not to fire until the enemy was twenty paces away. Fabrizio had twenty trees hastily felled, so that their branches completely blocked the narrow road. Captain Ranuccio, with five hundred men, shadowed the Orsini advance guard. Ranuccio had been ordered not to attack until he heard the first gunshots from the barrier of felled trunks.

When Fabrizio Colonna saw that his soldiers and peasants were well placed, each behind his tree and braced for battle, he left at a gallop with his mounted men, among them Giulio Branciforte. The prince took a path to the right of the main road, which led to the end of the clearing.

They had barely set off when a large troop of riders appeared on the road from Valmontone. It was the secret police and Orsini's horsemen escorting Baldassare Bandini. In their midst rode the prisoner, surrounded by four executioners dressed in red. They had been ordered to put Bandini to death if they thought Colonna's partisans might be about to rescue him.

Colonna's cavalry had just reached the edge of the clearing when the prince heard the first gunshots from the ambush he had set on the main road in front of the barricade. At once he and his cavalry charged towards the four executioners who surrounded Bandini.

The battle lasted but three-quarters of an hour. Taken by surprise, Orsini's followers scattered in all directions. In Colonna's advance guard, brave Captain Ranuccio was killed, a misfortune that had tragic consequences for Branciforte. As he fought his way towards the executioners, Giulio came face to face with Fabio Campireali.

Mounted on a foaming horse and clothed in a gilded *giacca*, Fabio shouted, 'Who are these wretched creatures? Let's slash their masks. Watch how I do it.'

A sword caught Giulio Branciforte across the forehead. The blow was so skilfully aimed that his hood slipped down and he was blinded by blood. So as to catch his breath and wipe his face, Giulio tugged his horse aside. Anxious to avoid an encounter with

Elena's brother, he had retreated a few paces when he received a sharp sword thrust to the chest. Thanks to his *giacca* the point did not penetrate, but he was momentarily winded. Almost at once he heard a cry in his ear.

'*Ti conosco, porco!* Swine, I know you! This is how you earn the money to replace your rags.'

Sorely angered, Giulio forgot his first resolve and turning to Fabio he shouted, '*Ed in mal punto tu venisti!* You've come at a bad moment.'

Several exchanges of sword thrusts shredded the garments which covered their mail. Fabio's armour was gilded and sumptuous, Giulio's plain.

'Fom what sewer did you scavenge that *giacca*?' shouted Fabio.

Just then, Giulio saw his opportunity. Fabio's splendid coat of mail was loose round his neck, and Giulio's sword found a gap. Its point sank half a foot into Fabio's throat, and a great jet of blood spurted out.

'Impudent fellow,' shouted Giulio, and he galloped towards the men in red, two of whom were still on horseback a hundred paces away. As he approached them, one fell, but just as Giulio reached the last remaining executioner, the man, finding himself surrounded by more than ten horsemen, fired his pistol point blank at the unfortunate Baltassare Bandini.

'There's no more we can do here, my friends,'

called out Branciforte. 'Let's carve up the cowardly police who ran off.'

His men followed him.

When half an hour later Giulio returned to Fabrizio, the prince addressed him for the first time ever. Giulio thought Prince Colonna would be greatly pleased by the victory, which was total and due entirely to his own skill, for Orsini had nearly three thousand men and Fabrizio only fifteen hundred. But Colonna was drunk with rage.

'We have lost our true friend Ranuccio,' he cried. 'I have just laid my hand on his body. It's already cold. Poor Baldassare Bandini is mortally wounded. So we've really lost. But the shade of brave Captain Ranuccio will appear before Pluto well accompanied. I've ordered all these prisoners, this scum, to be hanged from the trees. Do not fail in this, men!'

He galloped off to where the battle of the advance guard had taken place. With the remnants of Ranuccio's band Giulio followed the prince, who found the body of the old soldier surrounded by more than fifty enemy dead. The prince dismounted and once more took Ranuccio's hand. Weeping, Giulio did likewise.

'You are very young,' said the prince to Giulio, 'but I see you are covered in blood. Your father was a brave man who was wounded more than twenty times in the service of the Colonna family. Take command of Ranuccio's band and bear his body to our church in La Petrella. Remember, you may be set upon along the way.'

Giulio was not attacked but he stabbed to death one of his own soldiers who said he was too young to be a commander. This rash act passed censure because Giulio was still covered in Fabio's blood. All along the road he found trees laden with hanged men. This repulsive sight, together with Ranuccio's death – and above all Fabio's – nearly drove Giulio mad. His only hope was that no one knew the name of Fabio's killer.

Three days after the battle, Giulio returned to Albano. He told his friends that a high fever had kept him in Rome, where he'd spent the whole week in bed. But everywhere he was approached with marked respect. The most important people in the town were the first to greet him. Some rash persons went so far as to address him as Signor Capitano. On several occasions he passed by the Palazzo Campireali, which was completely closed up. But as the new young captain was shy about asking certain questions, it was not until midday that he brought himself to approach Scotti, who had always been kind to him. 'Where are the Campireali?' Giulio asked. 'Their palazzo is locked up.'

'My friend,' replied the grief-stricken Scotti, 'theirs is a name you must never utter. Your friends are convinced it was Fabio who sought your life and they will say this anywhere, but really he was the main hindrance to your marriage. His death leaves an extremely wealthy sister, who is in love with you. Add to this – and here indiscretion is to your advantage – that she loves you enough to make nightly trysts with you at your house. That means that you and she were husband and wife before the fateful battle.'

Seeing Giulio begin to weep, the old man fell silent.

'Let's go to the inn,' said Giulio.

Scotti followed. They were given a room, which they entered and locked, and Giulio asked permission to tell the old man everything that had happened the previous week.

When the long story ended, the old man said, 'I can see by your tears that none of what you did was premeditated. But Fabio's death is nonetheless a disastrous accident for you. Elena must tell her mother that you have been married for a long time.'

Giulio did not reply, which the old man put down to a praiseworthy discretion. Absorbed in deep thought, the young man wondered whether Elena would be too upset by her brother's death to appreciate Giulio's own grief. He cursed what had happened.

Then at Giulio's request, the old man recounted all that had taken place in Albano on the day of the battle. Although Fabio had been killed at half-past six in the morning, more than six leagues from Albano, by nine o'clock his death was already known. Towards midday old Campireali had been seen weeping, supported by his servants, on his way to the Capuchin monastery. Shortly after, three of the good fathers, mounted on the best Campireali steeds and followed by many servants, were journeying to the village of Ciampi, near where the battle took place. Old Campireali had insisted on following, but he had been persuaded not to because Fabrizio Colonna was furious – no one knew exactly why – and might well harm him if he were captured.

That evening, towards midnight, all Faggiola forest seemed ablaze. It was the monks and the poor people of Albano, carrying lighted brands, going to meet young Fabio's corpse.

'I will not hide from you', went on the old man, dropping his voice as if afraid of being overheard, 'that the road leading to Valmontone and Ciampi . . .'

'Well?' said Giulio.

'Well, this road passes in front of your house, and it is said that when Fabio's body reached that point blood spurted from his fearful wound.'

'Terrible, terrible!' cried Giulio, starting to his feet.

'Calm yourself, my friend,' said the old man. 'You must see that you need to know everything. I think you may have come back too soon. If you would do me the honour of asking my advice, I would add, Captain, that you should stay away from Albano for at least a month. I don't have to tell you that it would not be wise for you to be seen in Rome either. No one yet knows what the Holy Father will do to Prince Colonna. It is thought that he will uphold Fabrizio's claim that he only heard of the battle of Ciampi by rumour. But the governor of Rome, who is one of the Orsini camp, is furious and would like nothing better than to hang some of Fabrizio's soldiers, at which the prince can hardly complain since he swears he had no involvement in the battle. I shall go further and take the liberty of giving you military advice. You are well liked in Albano, otherwise you would not be safe here. You've been walking about the town for several hours. One of Orsini's men might think he was being insulted or that it would be easy to get his hands on a fine reward. Old Campireali has said a thousand times that he'll give his best land to the man who kills you. You ought to send some of the soldiers in your house down to Albano.'

'I have no soldiers in my house.'

'In that case, Captain, you are mad. This inn has a garden. We'll leave that way and cut across the vineyard. I'll come with you; I am old and unarmed. But, if we meet any enemies I'll speak to them and that should gain you some time.'

Giulio was in despair. What madness had he in mind? After learning that the Palazzo Campireali was empty and all its inhabitants had left for Rome, he had decided to go back to see the garden where he'd enjoyed so many trysts with Elena. He even hoped to revisit her room, where he'd been welcomed when Elena's mother was away. He needed to steady himself to face her anger by seeing once more the places where she'd been so tender to him.

Branciforte and the old man met no enemies as they followed the little paths that cut through the vineyard and climbed towards the lake.

Giulio wanted to hear again the details of Fabio's funeral. Escorted by many priests, the body of the young man had been taken to Rome and buried in the family vault at the Monastery of Sant' Onofrio, on the summit of the Janiculum. On the eve of the ceremony, strangely, Elena had been taken back to the Convent of the Visitation in Castro. This confirmed the rumours that she had been secretly married to the soldier of fortune who'd had the ill luck to kill her brother.

When he neared his house, Giulio met the corporal of his company and four of his soldiers. They told him that their late captain never left the forest without taking some of his men with him. Prince Colonna often said that if anyone wanted to get himself killed through recklessness he must first tender his resignation so as not to oblige the prince to avenge a death.

Giulio Branciforte now understood the justice of this remark, which previously had been obscure to him. Hitherto he had thought that war consisted solely of fighting courageously. There and then he obeyed the prince's orders, only allowing himself time to embrace the wise old man who had been kind enough to see him home.

A few days later, half crazed with melancholy, Giulio returned to the Palazzo Campireali. At dusk, he and three soldiers, disguised as Neapolitan merchants, entered Albano. He went alone to Scotti's house, where he learned that Elena was still in the Convent of Castro. Her father, who thought she was married to his son's murderer, had sworn never to see her again. He had not even looked at her while escorting her to the convent. Conversely, her mother's affection had further increased, and she often left Rome to spend a day or two with her daughter.

IV

'If I cannot justify my actions to Elena,' thought Giulio that night on reaching his company's camp in the forest, 'she'll think me a murderer. God knows what she's been told about the battle.'

He went to the fortress of La Petrella to receive orders from Prince Colonna and asked him for leave to go to Castro.

Fabrizio Colonna frowned. 'The matter of that little battle has not yet been settled with His Holiness,' he said. 'I have to tell you that I spoke the truth, which is that I knew nothing about the engagement, as news of it only reached me here the following day. I've reason to believe His Holiness will accept my account. The Orsini are powerful, but everyone says you distinguished yourself in the affray. The Orsini are even claiming that some of the prisoners were hanged from trees. You know that simply is not true, but we can expect reprisals.'

The astonishment on the naive young captain's face amused the prince. However, because of it, Colonna decided to explain himself more fully.

'I see in you the immense courage that made the

name of Branciforte known throughout Italy,' the prince went on. 'I hope you'll prove as faithful to my family as your dear father was, and I want to reward you for this. These are the rules of my organization. Never speak the truth about anything concerning me or my soldiers. If at any time you are forced to speak and you do not see any point in lying, tell any sort of falsehood but refrain as from mortal sin from speaking the truth. You must understand that it could give away all my plans. I know of your little affair in the Convent of the Visitation. You can spend two weeks in Castro, but the Orsini will certainly have friends and even spies there. Go to my steward. He'll give you two hundred *zecchini*. The friendship I enjoyed with your father', added the prince, laughing, 'makes me want to offer you some advice on the proper way to conduct your amorous skirmish. You and three soldiers will disguise yourselves as merchants. You'll pretend to be angry with your companions, who will pretend to be drunk and will make many friends by buying wine for all the layabouts in Castro. Further,' added the prince in a different tone, 'if you're captured and killed by the Orsini, do not let your real name be known. Above all, never admit you're one of my men. I don't need to tell you to give a wide berth to small settlements and always enter a town by the gate opposite to the direction from which you are travelling.'

Giulio was overwhelmed by this fatherly advice,

coming from such a normally stern man. At first the prince smiled at the tears he saw in the young man's eyes. Then his tone changed. He slipped off one of his many rings. Taking it, Giulio kissed the hand renowned for so many illustrious deeds.

'My father never spoke to me like this,' the young man said fervently.

Two days later, a little before dawn, Giulio entered the town of Castro. Five soldiers, also disguised, accompanied him. Two came separately and pretended not to know him or the other three. While approaching the town, Giulio had observed the Convent of the Visitation, a huge fortress-like structure rising above dark surrounding walls. He headed straight for the sumptuous church. The nuns, who were all from noble and mostly rich families and were full of pride and self-esteem, competed with each other to enrich the church, the only part of the convent open to the public. The custom was for one of these ladies, appointed abbess by the pope from a list of three names presented by the cardinal, protector of the Order of the Visitation, to make a very large donation in order to preserve her name for posterity. If her offering was smaller than that of the previous abbess, she and her family would be held in disregard.

Astonished, Giulio made his way along the nave of the magnificent building, with its gilding and its marble statues. He had little thought for either. He felt as if Elena were watching him. The high altar was said to have cost more than eight hundred thousand scudi, but blind to its splendour he fixed his eyes on a golden grille nearly forty feet high and divided in three by two marble columns. Menacing in its size, the grille rose behind the high altar, separating the nun's choir from the church.

Behind this grille nuns and boarders sat during the services. There they could come and pray at any time of day. It was on this well-known fact that Giulio had placed his hopes.

A huge black curtain covered the inside of the grille but did not conceal the boarders' view of the public. Through the curtain Giulio could clearly see the windows which lit up the choir and he could make out even the smallest detail. Each bar of the magnificent grille bore a sharp spike turned towards the congregation.

Giulio chose a conspicuous position in the best-lit area. Here he spent his time attending Masses. Noting that he was surrounded only by peasants and hoping he would be observed from the other side of the black curtain, for the first time in his life he tried to attract attention to himself. His plan was carefully thought out. He gave copious alms both on entering and leaving the church. He and his men showed interest in all the workmen and small traders who had business with the convent.

It was not until the third day that he at last became hopeful of getting a letter to Elena. On his orders his men followed the lay sisters who bought some of the convent's provisions. One of them had dealings with a tradesman. A soldier of Giulio's, who had been a monk, befriended the tradesman and promised him a *zecchino* for each letter he delivered to the boarder Elena Campireali.

'What,' said the tradesman, when first approached, 'take a letter to the brigand's wife?'

So fast does gossip travel that, although Elena had only been in Castro for two weeks, her fame was already established.

'At least she's married!' the tradesman added. 'How many of our ladies haven't that excuse and get much more than letters from outside.'

In his first missive Giulio gave a painstaking description of all that had happened on the fateful day of Fabio's death. 'Do you hate me?' he finished.

Elena replied, saying that without hating anyone she proposed to spend the rest of her life trying to forget him by whose hand her brother had perished.

Giulio hastened to write again. After cursing fate he said:

You wish then to forget the word of God revealed to us in the Holy Scriptures? God says, 'A woman shall leave her mother and father and cleave unto her husband.' Do you claim you are not my wife? Remember St Peter's Night as dawn broke behind Monte Cavo, and you threw yourself at my feet. You were mine if I wished to take you; you could not hold back the love

you then felt for me. Suddenly it seemed to me that, because
I had often told you that a long time ago I sacrificed to you
my life and everything I hold dearest in the world, you could
have said, but never did, that all that sacrifice, unmarked by
any act, could well be imaginary. A notion, to my mind cruel
but basically just, struck me. I saw it was not for nothing that
fate offered me the opportunity to sacrifice for you the greatest
happiness I could ever dream of. You were already defence-
less in my arms; even your mouth dared not refuse. Just then
the morning Ave Maria rang out in the Monte Cavo Monastery, and, by strange chance, the sound reached us. You said,
'Make this sacrifice to the Madonna, the mother of purity.'
The idea of this supreme sacrifice, the only real one I would
ever have the chance to make to you, had already occurred to
me. I found it curious that the same thought came to you. The
distant sound of that Ave Maria touched me, I admit, and I
gave in to what you asked. The sacrifice was not wholly for
you; I wanted to place our future union under the Madonna's
protection. At that time I thought the obstacles came not from
you but from your rich, noble family. If there had been no
supernatural cause, how did that Angelus reach us from so far
away, over the treetops of half the forest, stirred by the morning
breeze? Then, remember, you fell at my feet; I took from my
breast the cross I wear and you swore on it, by your everlasting
damnation, that wherever you were, whatever was happening,
as soon as I ordered you would be entirely mine just as you
were when we heard the distant Ave Maria from Monte Cavo.
Then we both devoutly said two Aves and two Paters. Well! By
the love you had for me or, if you have forgotten it – as I fear

– by your eternal damnation, I order you to receive me tonight in your room or in the convent garden.

After many more exchanges, Elena eventually complied. Giulio found a way of getting into the convent disguised as a woman. Elena received him, but only at the grille of a window on the ground floor overlooking the garden. To his inexpressible grief, Giulio found the young girl, who had once been so tender and passionate, now like a stranger. She treated him with polite formality. In letting him into the garden, she had yielded solely to the letter of the oath. They spoke briefly, and after a few seconds Giulio's pride, perhaps somewhat excited by what had happened over the past fortnight, outweighed his deep sorrow.

'I see nothing before me,' he said under his breath, 'but the grave of that Elena who, in Albano, seemed to have given herself to me for life.'

Now Giulio was hard put to it to hide the tears that Elena's formal manner had brought to his eyes. When she finished speaking, justifying what she described as a natural change of heart after a brother's death, Giulio spoke gently.

'You're not fulfilling your oath,' he said. 'You're not meeting me in a garden and you are not on your knees before me as you were half a minute after we heard the Ave Maria from Monte Cavo. Forget your oath if you can. For my part, I forget nothing. May God help you!'

With these words, Giulio left the window grille, where he had been for nearly an hour. Who would have thought he'd cut short a conversation he had so long desired? The act wrenched his soul, but he felt that if he replied to her empty words except by leaving her with her remorse he would further deserve her scorn.

He left the convent before daybreak. At once he mounted his horse, ordering the soldiers to wait for him there in Castro for another week and then return to the forest. Drunk with despair, he set off for Rome.

'So now I am leaving her,' he kept saying to himself. 'We've become strangers. Oh, Fabio, how you are avenged!'

The sight of men at work along the way irritated him. He spurred his horse over the fields and towards the desolate seashore. Once he had passed the peacefully labouring peasants, whose lot he envied, he breathed again. The wildness of the sea matched his despair and lessened his anger. Now he could give in to his sad fate.

'My only way out of this is to to fall in love with another woman,' he thought.

At this melancholy idea, his despair redoubled. There was but one woman in the world for him. Imagining the torments he would suffer if he dared speak the word love to anyone but Elena, he broke into bitter laughter.

'I'm like one of Ariosto's heroes, travelling alone

through deserted lands after finding his treacherous mistress in the arms of another knight,' Giulio thought. 'At least Elena's not guilty of that. Her faithlessness is owed not to her loving another but to the fact that her soul was driven mad by the terrible things she was told about me. I'm sure her family made it look as if I only joined that doomed expedition hoping secretly for the chance to kill her brother. What's more, they probably accused me of the sordid calculation that once her brother was dead she would become sole heir to a vast fortune. And I was foolish enough to leave her for two whole weeks, a prey to my enemies' lies. I seem to have lost the ability to direct my own life. I'm a fool, a contemptible fool. My life is no use to me or anyone else.'

He was riding along the tideline, his horse's hooves occasionally washed by a wavelet. If he were to urge the animal into the sea he could put an end to the anguish that gripped him. What did life hold now that the one person in the world who gave him happiness had deserted him? But his thoughts ran on.

'What is this agony compared with that I will suffer for ever once this wretched life is over? Elena will not only be indifferent to me as she now is but I will also see her in the arms of a rival, some rich, well-connected young Roman. To tear my soul, the demons of hell, as is their duty, will find the cruellest pictures. Thus even in death I will not be able to forget Elena. On the contrary, my passion for her will grow because it would be the best way for the powers of eternity to punish me for my heinous sin.'

To rid himself of the temptation, Giulio devoutly recited the Ave Maria. It was while hearing the morning Ave Maria that he had been drawn into a generous act which he now looked on as the greatest error of his life. But he dared reflect no further on this notion.

'If out of faith in the Madonna I have made a tragic mistake, should she not through her infinite mercy find some way to restore my happiness?'

Contemplating the Madonna's mercy gradually drove away Giulio's despair. He raised his head and before him, behind Albano and the forest, he saw Monte Cavo in its dark green mantle and the monastery whose morning Ave had brought him to what he called his infamous betrayal. The sudden sight of this holy place consoled him.

'No,' he cried, 'the Madonna cannot possibly desert me. If Elena were my wife, as she in her love for me desired and I in my manly honour wished, the story of her brother's death would have found in her soul the memory of the tie that bound her to me. She would have told herself that she was mine long before the mischance that brought me face to face with Fabio on the battlefield. Two years older than I, he was more experienced in the use of arms and bolder, stronger in every way. A thousand reasons could have proven to my wife that it was not I who sought that encounter. She would have remembered that I never expressed the slightest feeling of hatred for her brother, even when he fired on her. I remember that at our first meeting, after my return from Rome, I said to her, "What do you want me to do? Honour demanded it. I cannot fault a brother.'"

Hope restored through his devotions to the Madonna, Giulio urged his horse on and in a few hours reached his company's camp, where the men were arming themselves. They were about to set off for Rome via Monte Cassino. The young captain changed horses and rode with his soldiers. They did not fight that day. Giulio did not ask why they were marching; he did not care. As soon as he was at the head of his band he began to see his destiny in a different light.

'I must be a fool,' he thought. 'I was wrong to leave Castro. Elena is probably less guilty than I imagined in my anger. That innocent soul in whom I saw the birth of love cannot have ceased to belong to me. She was filled with such passion for me! Did she not offer more than ten times to run away with me, poor as I am, and get a monk from Monte Cavo to marry us? In Castro, I should have arranged a second meeting and reasoned with her. Truly passion makes me childish! Oh God! If only I had someone to turn to. Each course of action I contemplate seems perfect at first and two minutes later disastrous.'

That evening, as they left the high road to plunge back into the forest, Giulio went to the prince and asked if he could stay on a few more days at Castro.

'Go to the devil,' cried Colonna. 'I've no time for infantile nonsense.'

An hour later Giulio set out for Castro. There he met his men again but he was not sure how to write to Elena after he'd left her in such a haughty way. His first letter read only, 'May I see you tomorrow night?'

'You may,' came the reply.

After Giulio had left her, Elena felt more rejected than ever. Then she began to understand the poor young man's state of mind. She was his wife before he had the ill luck to meet her brother in battle.

This time Giulio was not received with the formal courtesies which had seemed so cruel at his earlier meeting. Elena again appeared behind her barred window, but she was trembling. Giulio's tone was reserved, and he spoke almost as if to a stranger. Now it was Elena's turn to suffer the cruelty of a formal voice, which had once held only the tenderest intimacy. Fearing that his soul would be rent by a single cold word from Elena, Giulio claimed in the tone of a lawyer that Elena was his wife well before the battle of Ciampi.

She let him speak, as she was afraid of being overcome by tears if she uttered more than a brief response. In the end, feeling she was about to break down, she made Giulio agree to come back the next day, as that night, the eve of an important feast day, matins would be sung early and their assignation would be discovered. Giulio left the garden deep in thought, unable to make up his mind whether he had been well or badly received.

But then, prompted by conversations with his fellow soldiers, the idea of using force took root in his head. 'One day I may have to come and carry Elena off,' he told himself, and he began to work out ways of breaking into the garden.

The convent was very wealthy and very good at extorting money. In its pay it had a large house-hold of mostly veteran soldiers, who were lodged in a barracks with barred windows. These windows overlooked a narrow passage that ran from the outer portal of the convent and cut through a towering wall to an inner door that was in turn watched over by the nun in attendance.

On one side of the narrow passage rose the bar-racks, on the other the thirty-foot-high garden wall. The convent façade faced the town square. It was a rough, age-blackened wall, with no openings but an outer door and a single small window through which the soldiers could peer. Set inside this grim wall was an inner door reinforced by a wide sheet of steel fastened with huge nails. Above was a tiny window four feet high by eighteen inches wide.

In their conversations the lovers fell back into a

tone as intimate as it had been in Albano. Elena, however, refused to go into the garden. One night she was deeply pensive. Her mother had come from Rome to see her and had taken lodgings in the convent for a few days. Devoted to her daughter, she had always been able to show Elena her affection with such subtlety that the girl immediately felt guilty at having to deceive her. How could she tell her mother that she was receiving the man who had taken her son from her?

In the end, Elena confessed to Giulio that if her mother pressed her she would not have the courage to lie. Giulio realized the risk he was running. His fate hung on a chance word from Signora de' Campireali.

'Tomorrow I'll come earlier,' he said on the following night. 'I'll remove one of the bars from this grille, you will come down into the garden, and I'll take you to a church in town where a priest who is a close friend will marry us. Before daybreak you'll be back in this garden. Once you are my wife I shall no longer be afraid, and, if your mother demands that I atone for the tragedy we all equally deplore, I'll agree to anything, even to going several months without seeing you.'

As Elena seemed horrified by this suggestion, Giulio added, 'The prince has recalled me to his side. Honour demands that I go. What I have suggested is the only way we can have a future. If you do not agree, we shall part for ever, here and now. I'll leave with remorse for my rashness. I took you at your word. If you break our sacred vow, I hope that one day I will find it in me to despise you for the way you have played with me. Perhaps then I'll be cured of this love which has brought such agony to my life.'

'Oh God, how terrible for my mother,' Elena cried, in tears.

Finally she agreed to his suggestion but then she added, 'We might be caught on the way there or back. Think of the scandal. Think of the awful position my mother will be in. Let's wait a few days until she leaves.'

'You are making me doubt what I once held dearest – my trust in your word. Tomorrow evening we shall be married or we shall meet for the last time on this side of the grave.'

Poor Elena could only reply with tears. She was devastated by Giulio's brutal, determined voice. Did she really deserve his contempt? Was he the same lover who had been so gentle and shy? At last she agreed to his demand and Giulio left. In a state of extreme anxiety Elena waited for nightfall. Had she been expecting certain death her sorrow could not have been keener. The night passed in an agony of indecision. There were moments when she wanted to tell her mother everything. The next day Elena looked so pale that her mother forgot all the wise counsel she intended to give and threw her arms round her daughter.

'What has happened?' she cried. 'Oh God, tell me what you've done or what you're about to do. If you plunge a dagger into my heart, I'll suffer less than by your cruel silence.'

Elena saw from her mother's words that rather than exaggerate her feelings she was trying to temper them. The girl's soft heart was won over. She fell to her knees. As her mother sought to discover the daughter's fateful secret, sobbing that Elena was about to flee from her, the girl replied that the next and all the following days she would stay with her mother, but she begged her to demand no more.

This rash remark was soon followed by a full confession. Signora de' Campireali was appalled to find that her son's killer was so near. But her grief gave way to a surge of pure joy. Her delight was complete when she saw that her daughter had never failed in her duty.

At that, the mother's cunning schemes changed entirely. She felt justified in plotting against a man who meant nothing to her. Elena's heart was torn. Her sincerity could not have been greater. Conscience-racked, her soul needed soothing. Signora de' Campireali came up with a long series of justifications. She easily convinced her anguished daughter that rather than stain her reputation by a furtive ceremony, Elena could marry openly and honourably if she were to postpone for a week the obedience she owed to her generous lover.

Signora de' Campireali would leave for Rome, where she would reveal to her husband that long before the battle of Ciampi Elena had been married to Giulio. The ceremony had taken place on the night when, wearing a monk's habit, she had met her father and brother near the Capuchin monastery. All that day the mother was careful not to leave her daughter alone, and in the evening Elena wrote a touching letter to her lover in which she described the torment tearing her heart in two and implored him to wait for another week.

As I write this letter, which my mother's messenger will deliver, I believe I was wrong to tell her all. I know you will be angry and I can feel the hate in your eyes. My heart is torn by bitter remorse. You will say I am weak, mean-spirited, contemptible. I know this, my dear angel. But imagine what I had to witness — my mother in tears, beseeching me. I could not help telling her that there was a reason for my silence. Once I fell into the weakness of speaking so unwisely, I felt obliged to recount all that had happened between you and me. Drained of its strength, my soul needed counsel. I had hoped to receive it from my mother. I forgot, my dear, that the interests of my beloved mother are opposed to yours. I forgot my first duty, which is to obey you. Perhaps I am incapable of feeling that true love which overcomes all trials. Despise me, my Giulio, but in God's name do not stop loving me. Take me away if

Pescara and Chieti, ordering the farmers to send to Castro some faithful men, able and willing to carry out an assassination. She did not hide from them that it was to avenge the death of Fabio, their young master.

V

But two days later Giulio was back in Castro with eight soldiers who were willing to follow him and face the prince's anger. Prince Colonna sometimes had men put to death for the kind of enterprise Giulio was about to undertake. He already had five men in Castro, but the convent was like a fortress, and fourteen soldiers, however brave, seemed too few for the venture.

By skill or force they had to breach the convent's outer door. They then had to make their way down a fifty-yard-long passage. On one side rose the barred windows of the barracks, where the nuns had installed their thirty or forty veteran soldiers, or *bravi*. From these windows a withering fire would come as soon as the alarm sounded.

The present abbess, who was a foolish woman, feared the activities of the Orsini overlords, Prince Colonna, Marco Sciarra, and all the others who were chieftains in the region. How could her men prevent eight hundred resolute brigands from unexpectedly taking over a small town like Castro, knowing the convent was full of gold?

The wall on the right of the passage was too high to scale. At the end was an iron door that opened onto a colonnaded hall. Here was the convent's main courtyard and then its garden. The iron door was guarded by a gatekeeper nun.

When Giulio and his men came within three leagues of Castro, they halted in the heat of the day at an inn set back from the road. There he explained his plan, sketching in the sand a layout of the convent.

'At nine o'clock,' he told his men, 'we will eat outside the town. At midnight we'll enter it. There we will meet your five comrades, who are waiting near the convent. One of them, who'll be on horseback, will pretend to be a courier from Rome come to bring Signora de' Campireali to her husband, who is dying. We will try to get through the first door here in the middle of the barracks without a sound.' He pointed to the drawing in the sand. 'If we start to fight at the outer door, the *bravi* will simply fire on us while we are in this little square in front of the convent or while we're moving down this narrow passage leading to the inner door. This second door is iron, but I have a key to it.

'Heavy iron bars are fixed to the wall with bolts. When in place these bolts prevent the two sections of the door from opening. But, as the bars are too massive for the gatekeeper to move, I have never seen them in place and I've been through that door ten times or more. I'm sure we'll manage it without any trouble. You know I have spies in the convent. I intend to carry off a boarder, not a nun. We shall use weapons only as a last resort. If we have to fight before we reach the barred door, the nun at the gate will summon one of the seventy-year-old gardeners who live in the convent, and one of these old men will pull the iron bolts to. In that event we'll have to break down the wall, which will take ten minutes. In any case I shall approach the door first. One of the gardeners is in my pay, but I've been careful to tell him nothing of my plan. Once past this second door, we shall turn right into the garden. Here's where the fighting will start. We must kill anyone we meet, but only with sword and rapier, as the slightest gunshot will wake the whole town, who'll be sure to set on us as we leave. With thirteen men like you, I'll be able to fight my way through this sleepy town. No one will dare come down into the streets, but many of the townspeople have arquebuses and will fire from their windows. If so, we must slip along the walls of the houses. Once in the convent garden, you will quietly order anyone who appears to get back and use your rapiers on anyone who doesn't obey at once. I'll climb into the convent by the garden door with those of you nearest me. Three minutes later, I'll bring out either one woman or two, whom we'll carry in our arms. Then we'll leave the convent and the town at high speed. I'll station two of you by the door, and you'll fire twenty shots at minute intervals to scare off the people.

'Is all this clear?' Giulio asked. 'It'll be dark in the entrance hall. The garden is to the right, the court-yard to the left. Don't get it wrong.'

'Count on us!' cried the soldiers.

Then they went drinking. The corporal stayed behind and asked for a word with Giulio.

'Nothing could be simpler than Your Honour's plan,' he said. 'I've broken into two convents in my time, but there are too few of us for this one. If we have to tear down that wall, the *bravi* in the bar-racks will not sit back and do nothing. They'll shoot seven or eight of us and they may snatch the women from us on our way out. That's what happened at a convent near Bologna. They killed five of us, and we killed eight of them, but the captain didn't get the woman. I have a couple of suggestions, Your Hon-our. I know four peasants who live near this tavern. They served bravely under Sciarra and for a single *zecchino* fought like lions all night. They may steal a bit of the convent's silverware, but what's that matter to you? That's up to them. You'll be paying them to get a woman, that's all. My second suggestion is this. Ugone is a skilful, educated fellow. He was a doctor but he took to the forest after killing his brother-in-law. You can send him to the convent door an hour before midnight. He'll ask for a job and will do it so well they'll put him in the guard. He'll get the nuns' servants drinking and then it will be easy for him to dampen the firing cords of their weapons.'

Unfortunately Giulio took the corporal's advice. As the man left, he added, 'We're breaking into a convent. This means absolute excommunication and, moreover, this convent is under the direct protection of the Madonna.'

'I understand,' replied Giulio, as if struck by this remark. 'Stay here with me.'

The corporal shut the door and came back to recite a rosary with Giulio. They prayed for an hour. At nightfall they set off.

On the stroke of midnight, Giulio, who had made his way alone into Castro at eleven o'clock, returned to the gate to fetch his men. He entered with his eight soldiers and three well-armed peasants. They joined the five already in the town. Thus Giulio found himself at the head of a resolute band of sixteen. Two were disguised as servants. They wore long black smocks to hide their mail and no feathers in their hats.

At half-past twelve, pretending to be the cardinal's courier, Giulio galloped up to the convent door and called loudly for them to open it. He was pleased to see that the soldiers, who replied through the little window beside the outer door, were quite drunk. As was the custom, he wrote his name on a piece of paper. A soldier took it to the nun who guarded the inner door and who had to wake the abbess. The reply took three long quarters of an hour, during which Giulio had difficulty keeping his men quiet. Some of the townspeople had even begun timidly to open their windows, when at last the abbess gave her consent.

Giulio climbed up to the guardroom by a short rope ladder let down from the little window, since the *bravi* did not want the bother of opening the main door. Two soldiers, disguised as servants, followed him. Leaping through the guardroom window, he came face to face with Ugone, who had plied all the guards with wine. Giulio told the captain of the guard that three servants of the Campireali household, who had been armed like soldiers to escort him on the road, had found some good brandy and he asked if they could come up, since they were getting bored down in the square. Everyone agreed. Giulio himself, with two men, went down the stairs from the guardroom to the passage.

'Try to open the main door,' he told Ugone.

He himself reached the iron door without difficulty. There he found the good gatekeeper nun, who told him that as it was past midnight if he entered the convent the abbess would have to write to the bishop. For this reason, she told him to give his dispatches to a little nun whom the abbess had sent to fetch them. Giulio replied that owing to the disorder following Signor de' Campireali's sudden decline, he had only a doctor's letter and he had to give the news

in person to the sick man's wife and daughter if these
ladies were still in the convent, or, in any case, to the
abbess. The nun went off with this message. This left
the young sister, the abbess's messenger, on her own
at the door. Chatting and joking with her, Giulio
slipped his hand through the iron bars of the door
and laughingly tried to open it. The nun, who was
very shy, took fright at the joke. Seeing that time
was going by, Giulio rashly offered her a handful of
zecchini to open the door for him, adding that he
was too tired to wait. At once he realized his mistake.
He should have resorted to cold steel rather than
gold but he didn't have the heart. Nothing would
have been simpler than to seize the girl, who was less
than a foot away from him on the other side of the
door. When he held out the coins the young nun
shrank back. She later said that from the way Giulio
spoke she could tell he was no plain courier. He is
the lover of one of our nuns, she thought, coming
for an assignation. She was a pious girl. Filled with
horror, she tugged as hard as she could at the rope of
a small bell in the main courtyard, which immediately
made enough din to waken the dead.

'This is it,' said Giulio to his men, 'Look to yourselves.'

He took his key, and putting an arm through the
iron bars, he opened the door. The young nun fell
on her knees in dismay and began to babble Ave
Marias and cry, 'Sacrilege.' Again Giulio should have

silenced her, but he could not bring himself to. One of his men grabbed the girl and put a hand over her mouth.

Just then, someone fired an arquebus in the passageway. Ugone had opened the main door. The rest of his soldiers were entering stealthily, when one of the *bravi*, less drunk than the others, glanced out of a barred window. Surprised to see so many men in the passage, he swore and ordered them to halt. Instead of ignoring him and continuing on to the iron door as the first soldiers had done, the last man, one of the peasants recruited that afternoon, fired at the guard calling down from the window and killed him. This shot and the shouts of the drunken guards when their comrade fell woke the convent soldiers, who had retired to bed that night without tasting Ugone's wine. Nine or ten *bravi* sprang half-dressed into the passage and threw themselves headlong at Branciforte's men.

Followed by his two soldiers, Giulio fled into the garden and ran to the door of the boarders' staircase. But there he was met by five or six pistol shots. His men both fell, and he took a bullet in the right arm. The shots were fired by Signora de' Campireali's bodyguard, who on her orders and with the bishop's permission were spending the night in the garden.

Giulio did his best to force the little door, but it was securely locked. He called to his men, but they lay dying. In the dark he came face to face with three

Campireali servants, whom he fought off with his dagger.

Running back through the entrance hall to call the rest of his men, Giulio found the iron door shut. The heavy bolts had been drawn and padlocked by the old gardeners, who'd been roused by the little nun's bell.

'I'm trapped,' he thought. He tried to force the chain with his rapier, hoping to reach one of the bars and break down a panel in the door. The weapon broke in a padlock. At that moment Giulio was wounded in the shoulder by one of the servants coming from the garden. He swung round, his back to the door, and was set upon by several men. He defended himself with his dagger. Luckily, as it was extremely dark, almost all the sword thrusts glanced off his mail coat. But he was badly wounded in the knee. Throwing himself at one of his assailants, who was too injured to wield his sword, Giulio lunged at the man's face with his dagger, felled him, and managed to snatch his weapon. He thought then he was safe. He placed himself at the garden side of the door. His men, who had run up, fired half a dozen shots through the iron bars of the door and sent the servants scattering. In the entrance hall nothing could be seen except by the flash of the pistol shots.

'Don't fire my way,' called out Giulio.

'You're caught like a rat in a trap,' replied the corporal calmly, speaking through the bars. 'Three of us are down. We're going to wrench the jamb on the other side of the door from you. Keep back. The bullets will fall on us. Have we enemies in the garden?'

'The wretched Campireali servants,' said Giulio.

He was still talking to the corporal when shots were fired at them from the garden. Giulio ducked into the porter's closet, where he found a dim lamp burning before a picture of the Madonna. Carefully, so as not to put it out, he took the lamp, noting with concern that his hands were shaking. His knee hurt and he examined it to find it was bleeding profusely.

Glancing round, he recognized a woman who lay in a wooden chair in a dead faint. It was Marietta, Elena's maid and confidante. He shook her sharply.

'What's this, Signor Giulio,' she cried out with a sob, 'are you going to kill your friend Marietta?'

'Far from it. Tell Elena I'm sorry to have disturbed her sleep and remind her of the Ave Maria of Monte Cavo. Here's a posy I picked in her garden at Albano. But there's blood on it. Wash it off before you give it to her.'

Just then a volley of arquebus shots rang out in the passage. The nuns' *bravi* were attacking his men.

'Where's the key to the little door?' he asked Marietta.

'I can't find it, but take these; they'll unlock the padlocks of the iron bars bolting the main door. You can get out.'

Giulio took the keys and dashed out of the room.

'There's no need to break down the wall,' he called to his soldiers. 'I've got the key.'

A short silence followed while he tried to open the padlocks. He had the wrong key. He tried another. It worked. But as he lifted the iron bar he was hit in the right arm at point-blank range. His arm fell to his side, useless.

'Lift the iron bar,' he called to his men.

He did not need to tell them. In the flash of a shot, they could see that the end of the bar was almost free. Three or four strong arms lifted the bar out, and let it fall. They pushed one of the double doors open, and the corporal went through.

'We can't go on,' he told Giulio in a low voice. 'Five of us are dead and only three or four uninjured.'

'I've lost blood,' replied Giulio, 'I think I'm going to pass out. Have them carry me away.'

As he spoke, the corporal was shot dead by the guards. By chance, Ugone had heard Giulio's order and summoned two soldiers to lift the captain. As Giulio was still conscious, he told them to carry him to the door at the foot of the garden. The soldiers cursed the order but obeyed.

'A hundred *zecchini* to whoever opens this door,' cried Giulio.

But the little door held firm. One of the old gardeners, stationed at a second-floor window, fired a volley of pistol shots, which revealed the soldiers' position.

After the failure to break down the door, Giulio fainted. Ugone told the soldiers to carry the captain away as fast as possible. He himself went into the porter's lodge and pushed little Marietta towards the door, ordering her harshly to save herself and never to say she had recognized him. Pulling the mattress off the bed, he smashed several chairs and set fire to the room. When it was ablaze, he took to his heels and fled through a hail of bullets fired by the convent's *bravi*.

More than a hundred and fifty yards from the Visitation, Ugone found the captain, now completely unconscious, being carried away. A minute or two later they were outside the town. Ugone called a halt. He had only four soldiers with him. Two he sent back into the town, ordering them to fire their weapons at five-minute intervals.

'Try and find your wounded comrades,' he said to them, 'and leave the town before daybreak. We'll follow the path from the Croce Rossa. Set fire to anything you can.'

When Giulio came to, they were three leagues from the town, and the sun was already high in the sky.

'You have only five men left, three of them wounded,' Ugone reported. 'Two peasants who survived have been rewarded with two *zecchini* and have now fled. I've sent the two unwounded men to a nearby town to find a surgeon.'

The surgeon, a shaky old man, soon arrived on a fine donkey. They'd had to threaten to set fire to his house to get him to come. He was so frightened he had to be given brandy to put him in a fit state to do anything. At last he began work. He told Giulio that his wounds were of no consequence.

'The knee is not serious,' he added, 'but you will limp all your life if you don't rest for the next two or three weeks.'

The surgeon bandaged the wounded soldiers. Ugone winked at Giulio, and they gave the surgeon two *zecchini*, at which he went into extravagant gestures of gratitude. Then, under the pretext of thanking him, they fed him so much brandy that he fell into a deep sleep. This was what they wanted. They carried him to a nearby field, wrapped four *zecchini* in a twist of paper, and put them in his pocket. It was the payment for his donkey, on which they put Giulio and one of the soldiers with a leg wound. They spent the midday heat in an ancient ruin on the edge of a small lake. They walked all night, avoiding villages, which were few and far between, and finally at dawn on the second day, Giulio, carried by his men, awoke in the depths of the Faggiola forest in the charcoal burner's hut that was his headquarters.

VI

The day after the battle, to their horror, the nuns of the Visitation found nine corpses in their garden and in the passageway which led from the outer to the inner door. Eight of their own *bravi* were wounded. Never had the convent known such fear. Gunshots had sometimes been fired in the square, but never such a number in the garden, in the heart of the building directly beneath the nuns' windows.

The incident had lasted a good hour and a half, and during this time the commotion had reached its climax inside the convent itself. If Giulio Branciforte had had a previous understanding with any of the nuns or boarders he would have succeeded. All he needed was for someone to have opened one of the many doors to the garden, but, carried away by indignation and anger at what he termed Elena's betrayal, Giulio wanted to take the convent by force. He would have thought he was failing in what he owed himself had he confided his plan to anyone who could have told it to Elena. But one word to little Marietta would have sufficed. She would have opened a door to the garden, and a single man appearing in the convent dormitories, while gunfire roared and raged outside, would have been obeyed to the letter. As soon as the shooting began, Elena had trembled for her lover's life and thought only of fleeing with him.

What must she have suffered when Marietta told her of Giulio's terrible wound, from which she had seen the blood pouring? Elena was appalled at what she felt was her cowardice. 'In a weak moment I confessed all to my mother, and Giulio's blood flowed. He might have been killed in this feat of daring and sheer courage.'

Admitted into the parlour, the *bravi* told the nuns that never in their lives had they witnessed such valour as that of the young man dressed as a courier, who led the brigands' attack. If the nuns listened with bated breath to these accounts, we can imagine the eagerness with which Elena asked the *bravi* for every last detail about the young chieftain. Having heard the lengthy accounts that she drew from them and from the old gardeners, all impartial witnesses, Elena no longer felt any love for her mother.

A few brief, violent words passed between the two women who on the eve of the skirmish had been so close. Signora de' Campireali was shocked at the bloodstains she noticed on a certain posy which Elena never set aside for a single moment.

'You must throw those spattered flowers away.'

'It was I who spilt this generous blood because I was weak enough to confide in you.'

'So you still love your brother's murderer?'

'I love my husband, who, to my everlasting regret, was set upon by my brother.'

After this, for the three days the mother remained at the convent, not another word passed between Signora de' Campireali and her daughter.

The day after her mother left, Elena managed to escape, taking advantage of the confusion which reigned at the convent's two entrances, where teams of stonemasons had been brought in to erect new fortifications. Elena and little Marietta disguised themselves as workmen, but the townspeople had mounted a heavy guard at Castro's gates. In a state of utter desperation Elena persuaded the tradesman who had smuggled Branciforte's letters to her to pretend she was his daughter and accompany her and her maid to Albano. There, at the home of her old nurse, who thanks to Elena's gifts had been able to open a small shop, the girl found refuge. She at once wrote to Branciforte, and, not without difficulty, the nurse found a man who agreed to risk entering the Faggiola forest without a pass from Colonna's soldiers.

Elena's messenger returned three days later, scared out of his wits. It had been impossible to find Branciforte, and then the many questions he'd asked about the young captain aroused suspicion, forcing him to flee.

'I'm certain Giulio is dead,' thought Elena, 'and that I killed him by my weakness and petty-mindedness.

He should have fallen in love with a strong woman, the daughter of one of Prince Colonna's captains.'

Fearing for Elena's life, the nurse climbed up to the Capuchin monastery that stood beside the rock-hewn path where Fabio and his father had once passed the two lovers in the middle of the night. The nurse spoke at length to her confessor, admitting to him in secret that young Elena de' Campireali wanted to join Giulio Branciforte, her husband, and that she was prepared to give the monastery chapel a silver lamp worth a hundred Spanish piastres.

'A hundred piastres!' replied the monk angrily. 'What will become of our monastery if we incur the wrath of Signor de' Campireali? He gave us not a hundred but a thousand piastres – as well as the candles – to fetch his son's body from the battlefield at Ciampi.'

It should be said in the monastery's defence that two elderly monks, who knew where Elena was hiding, went down to Albano with the initial intention of returning her, willingly or by force, to her family's palazzo. For this they knew they would be richly rewarded by Signora de' Campireali. All Albano hummed with gossip of Elena's flight and of the enormous rewards offered by her mother to anyone who could give her news of her daughter's where-abouts. But the two monks were so moved by poor Elena's despair over Giulio Branciforte's purported death that, far from betraying her, they agreed to escort her to La Petrella.

Still disguised as workmen, Elena and Marietta set off on foot by night to a certain spring in the Faggiola forest a league from Albano. There the monks had arranged for mules to be brought, and, when day came, they set off for La Petrella. The monks, who were known to enjoy the prince's protection, were greeted respectfully by the soldiers they met in the forest. But it was not so for the two young men the monks were escorting. The soldiers regarded them suspiciously, but approaching closer they burst out laughing and congratulated the Capuchins on the charm of their muleteers.

'Quiet, you blasphemers,' replied the monks, continuing their journey, 'and remember this is on the orders of Prince Colonna.'

But poor Elena was unlucky. The prince was away and when he returned three days later, at last consenting to see her, he was very harsh.

'Why have you come here, signorina?' he asked. 'What does this rash step mean? You gossiping women have caused the deaths of seven of the bravest men in Italy, and no reasonable man could ever forgive that. In this world you must either want something or not want it. Thanks most likely to your nonsense, Giulio Branciforte has just been declared guilty of sacrilege and condemned to have his flesh tortured for two hours by red-hot pincers and then burned alive like a Jew – him, one of the finest Christians I know. How, without some noxious gossip of yours, could such a horrible lie have been invented? What made people think that Giulio Branciforte was in Castro on the day the convent was attacked? My men will all tell you that they saw him in La Petrella that very day, and that evening I myself sent him to Velletri.'

'But is he alive?' cried Elena, bursting into tears for the tenth time.

'He is dead to you,' replied the prince. 'You will never see him again. I advise you to return to your convent. Try not to commit more foolish acts. I order you to leave La Petrella within the hour. Never tell a soul that you saw me or I will surely punish you.'

Poor Elena was heartbroken at such a reception by the renowned Prince Colonna, for whom Giulio had so much respect and whom she loved because Giulio loved him.

Despite what Prince Colonna said, Elena's action was not ill-advised. Had she reached La Petrella three days earlier, she would have found Giulio Branciforte. His knee wound had prevented him from walking, and the prince had him taken to Avezzano, a large town in the Kingdom of Naples. At the first news of the appalling judgement purchased by Signor de' Campireali, declaring Giulio guilty of sacrilege and violation of a convent, the prince saw that if it were to be a matter of protecting Branciforte he could not count on three-quarters of his men. A sin had been committed against the Madonna, whose protection every brigand regarded as his peculiar right. Had any chief constable from Rome dared penetrate the Faggiola forest to arrest Branciforte, he might well have succeeded.

Upon his arrival in Avezzano, escorted by trustworthy men, Giulio went by the name Fontana. When the men returned to La Petrella they announced with sorrow that Giulio had died on the journey, and from that moment on every one of the prince's soldiers knew he would receive a dagger in his heart if he uttered that ill-fated name.

Back in Albano, Elena vainly wrote letter after letter, spending every penny she had to have them taken to Branciforte. The two elderly monks who had become her friends – for Elena's great beauty never failed in its power, even conquering hearts hardened by selfishness and hypocrisy – advised the poor girl that she would never be able to get word to Branciforte. Prince Colonna had announced that he was dead, and Giulio would certainly not reappear in the world until the prince wished it. Elena's nurse told her, weeping, that her mother had managed to discover her hiding place, and strict orders had been given that she should be forcibly conveyed to the Palazzo Campireali. Elena knew that once in the palazzo she would be condemned to a confinement of the utmost rigidity and that she would be forbidden all communication with the outside world, while in the convent she would be able to send and receive letters just like other nuns. Moreover, and this was what prompted her decision, it was in the convent garden that Giulio had spilt his blood for her. There she would be able to see the gatekeeper's chair, where Giulio had rested for a moment to examine his knee wound. It was there he had given Marietta the blood-drenched posy that never left Elena's keeping.

She therefore returned sadly to the convent, and here, could we end her story, it would be a good thing for her as well as for the reader. Instead, we are to witness the lingering degradation of a noble and generous spirit. Carefully plotted measures and the lies of civilized society, which from then on beset Elena from all sides, now took the place of spontaneity and natural passion.

When a woman takes pains to acquire a pretty daughter, she thinks she has the right to direct the girl's life. At the age of six she is justly told, 'Child, straighten your ruff,' but when she is eighteen and her mother fifty – when the girl has more sense than the mother – the latter, carried away by the desire to control, still thinks she can run her daughter's life and even lie to her. We shall see that Vittoria Carafa, who, by a series of skilful, cleverly organized plots, brought about her cherished daughter's brutal death after twelve years of unhappiness was a sorry example of the obsessive need to dominate.

Before his death Signor de' Campireali had been pleased to see pronounced in Rome the sentence condemning Branciforte to two hours of torture in the main thoroughfares of the city and then to be burned on a slow fire and his ashes thrown into the Tiber. Frescoes in the cloisters of Santa Maria Novella, in Florence, still show how cruel sentences against those guilty of sacrilege were carried out. Usually a large company of guards was required to prevent the outraged people from taking over the executioner's office. Each person considered himself the Madonna's special friend. Signor de' Campireali had the sentence read to him again a moment or two before his death and he gave the lawyer who had procured the sentence his fine lands between Albano and the sea. This lawyer was by no means without skill. Branciforte was condemned to this appalling torture, yet no witness had come forward who had recognized him in the costume of the young courier who seemed to have such an authoritative command over the assailants. Signor de' Campireali's splendid gift outraged all the plotters in Rome. At the time there was at court a certain *fratone*, a learned monk so adept that he could even have forced the pope to confer upon him the cardinal's hat. This monk looked after Prince Colonna's affairs, and to the *fratone* this formidable client was worth great consideration. When Signora de' Campireali's daughter returned to Castro her mother sent for the *fratone*.

'Your Reverence, you will be generously rewarded for your help on a little matter I shall now explain to you. In a few days the sentence condemning Giulio Branciforte to torture is also to be published and made law in the Kingdom of Naples. I would ask Your Reverence to read this letter from the viceroy, who is distantly related to me and who deigns to give me this news. In what country can Branciforte find refuge? I intend to give fifty thousand piastres to the prince, all or part of which I shall beg him to give Giulio Branciforte on condition that he takes service with the King of Spain, my liege lord, against the Flemish rebels. The viceroy will give Branciforte a captain's brevet, and, so that the sentence passed on him for sacrilege – which I expect will also be applicable in Spain – should not end his career, he will bear the name Baron Lizzara, which is a small estate of mine in the Abruzzi. Meanwhile, in the form of a pretence sale, I will find a way to hand over the property to him. I doubt whether Your Reverence has ever seen a mother treat her son's killer so well. With five hundred piastres, we could long ago have got rid of the villain, but we have no desire to fall out with Colonna. So, be so good as to point out to him that my respect for his law is costing sixty to eighty thousand piastres. I never want to hear the name Branciforte again, but above all pay my respects to the prince.'

The *fratone* said that in the next three days he would be setting forth on a journey in the neighbourhood of Ostia, and Signora de' Campireali gave him a ring worth a thousand piastres.

A few days later the *fratone* returned to Rome and told Signora de' Campireali that he had not informed the prince of her proposition. However, within a month, young Branciforte would have left for Barcelona, where she could send him through the bankers of that town the sum of fifty thousand piastres.

Prince Colonna was having great difficulty with Giulio. Despite the dangers he ran in Italy, the young lover could not make up his mind to leave the country. The prince tried without success to point out to him that Signora de' Campireali might die. To no avail he promised that, in any event, after three years Giulio could return to his country. Giulio wept but would not agree. The prince had to order his departure as a service to his own person. Giulio could not refuse his father's friend, but more than anything he wanted to take orders from Elena. The prince agreed to have a long letter delivered, and, furthermore, he would allow Giulio to write to her once a month from Flanders. At last, the despairing lover left for Barcelona. All his letters were burned by the prince, who did not want Giulio ever to return to Italy. It should be added that, although far from being a conceited man, the prince believed that for the arrangement to have any chance of success he should say it was he who had decided to settle a small fortune of fifty thousand piastres on the only son of one of the Colonna family's most faithful servants.

Meanwhile, in the convent the unfortunate Elena was treated like a princess. Her father's death had put her in possession of a large fortune, and vast inheritances came down to her. As a result, she made a gift of five ells of black cloth to all the inhabitants of Castro and the surrounding area who wished to wear mourning for Signor de' Campireali. She was in the early days of mourning when someone unknown to her delivered a letter from Giulio.

It would be difficult to describe her emotions on opening this letter and her deep sadness on reading it. Yet it was indeed Giulio's handwriting. She examined it closely. The letter spoke of love, but – oh God – what sort of love! It was, of course, Signora de' Campireali who with great cunning had composed the missive. Her plan was to initiate a correspondence with seven or eight passionate love letters. Then she would prepare others, in which the love would seem gradually to fade away.

Ten years of unhappiness followed. Elena believed she had been completely forgotten. Nevertheless, she haughtily refused the courtship of the most illustrious young lords of Rome. Yet she had a moment of hesitation when Ottavio Colonna was mentioned. He was the eldest son of Fabrizio, who had given her such an unpleasant reception at La Petrella. It seemed to her that, if it were absolutely necessary that she take a husband to protect her lands in the Papal States and the Kingdom of Naples, she would find it less burdensome to bear the name of a man whom Giulio had loved. If she had agreed to this marriage, Elena would soon have discovered the truth about Giulio Branciforte. Old Prince Fabrizio often spoke, and with great enthusiasm, of the outstanding bravery of Colonel Lizzara, who, as with the heroes of ancient Rome, tried by daring deeds to distract his mind from the unhappy love affair that made all pleasures a mockery to him. He believed Elena had long since been married. He too had been inundated with Signora de' Campireali's lies.

Elena had partially reconciled herself with her cunning mother. Longing to see her daughter married, the signora begged her elderly friend Cardinal Santi Quattro, patron of the convent, who was on his way to Castro, to tell the older nuns in confidence that his visit had been delayed by an act of grace. The good Pope Gregory XIII, touched with pity for the soul of a brigand named Giulio Branciforte, who had in the past tried to violate their convent, had, on hearing of the brigand's death, wished to revoke the sentence declaring him guilty of sacrilege. His Holiness was convinced that with the burden of such a sentence Branciforte could never escape from purgatory. If, that was, captured and murdered by savages in Mexico during a revolt, Giulio had been lucky enough only to go to purgatory.

The news put the whole convent of Castro into a state of anxiety, Elena above all. By then she had given in to all the follies that great wealth can provoke in a person monumentally tired of life. From that moment on, she never left her room. So as to have her apartment in the little porter's lodge, where Giulio had taken refuge on the night of the battle, she had rebuilt half the convent. After considerable effort and something of a scandal, she had managed to trace and take into her service Branciforte's three surviving *bravi* out of the original five he had employed in the Castro assault. Among these was Ugone, now old and crippled by wounds. The appearance of these three men had caused much talk, but in the end the fear inspired by Elena's haughty character carried the day. Each morning, dressed in her livery, the men could be seen coming to the outer grille to receive her orders. Often they replied at length to her questions, which were always on the same subject.

After six months of solitude and withdrawal from the world, the first feeling that stirred Elena's spirit, broken as it was by irreversible tragedy and unending tedium, was one of vanity.

The abbess had recently died. As was normal practice, Cardinal Santi Quattro, still Patron of the Visitation at the advanced age of ninety-two, had drawn up a list of three nuns from which the pope was to choose the new abbess. Compelling reasons were required get His Holiness to read the last two names on the list. He usually crossed these off with a stroke of his pen, and the nomination was settled.

One day Elena was at the window of the erstwhile porter's lodge, which now formed the far end of the new wing she'd had built. This window was not more than two feet above the passage once washed with Giulio's blood and now part of the garden. The three nuns known for some hours to be on the cardinal's list had just passed the window where Elena sat, her eyes fixed on the ground. Not seeing the passers-by, she failed to greet them. Annoyed, one said quite loudly to the others, 'That's a fine way for a boarder to display her room to public view.'

Roused by these words, Elena lifted her eyes and met three spiteful looks.

'Well,' she thought, shutting the window without a word, 'I've been a lamb in this convent long enough. If only for the amusement of the townspeople, I must now be a wolf.'

An hour later one of Elena's men was sent with the following letter to her mother, who had been living in Rome for ten years and had there acquired considerable influence.

Most esteemed mother, every year on my birthday you give me three hundred thousand scudi. I spend this money honourably enough but on trivia. Although you no longer give me evidence of it, I know there are only two ways in which I can show my gratitude to you for all you have done on my behalf. I will never marry but I would be happy to become abbess of this convent. The idea came to me because the three ladies on

Cardinal Santi Quattro's list are enemies of mine. Whichever one is chosen, I expect to find myself in all kinds of difficulties. Give my birthday present to whomsoever you need to do what I ask. First, have the nomination put back six months, which will delight the prioress of the convent, who is my close friend and is now in charge. This in itself will bring me happiness, a word I can seldom use in reference to myself. My idea may sound mad, but, if you think there is any chance of success, in three days' time I will take the white veil. Eight years in the convent without a night spent elsewhere will give me the right to six months' exemption. The dispensation cannot be refused me, and will cost only forty scudi. I remain respectfully yours, esteemed mother, etc.

Signora de' Campireali was overjoyed by this letter. On receiving it, she bitterly repented having announced Branciforte's death to her daughter. She did not know how to end the deep depression into which her daughter had fallen. She dreaded some wild idea and even feared Elena might want to travel to Mexico, where Branciforte was supposedly killed, in which case it was highly likely that in Madrid she would learn Colonel Lizzara's real name. On the other hand, what her daughter was asking was perhaps the most difficult thing in the world and possibly the most absurd. A young girl who was not even a nun and moreover was only known for the mad passion a brigand had had for her, which she herself might well have returned, to be put at the head of a convent among whose members were relatives of all the Roman princes!

'But,' thought Signora de' Campireali, 'it is said that any case can be argued and therefore won.' In her reply, Vittoria Carafa gave her daughter hope. Elena's whims were usually capricious, but to make up for this she tired of them quickly. At an evening reception, gathering information on everyone from near or far who might have any link with the convent of Castro, Vittoria learned that her friend Cardinal Santi Quattro had been in a bad mood for the last few months. He wanted to marry his niece to Don Ottavio Colonna, Prince Fabrizio's eldest son. Instead, the prince was offering his second son, Don Lorenzo, because he needed to mend his fortunes, which were unexpectedly compromised by the war that the king of Naples and the pope, in alliance at last, were making on the brigands of the Faggiola forest. The prince's eldest son's wife would therefore need to bring a dowry of six hundred thousand piastres to the Colonna family. Even by disinheriting his other relatives in the most unforgivable way, Cardinal Santi Quattro could only offer a fortune of from three hundred and eighty thousand to four hundred thousand scudi.

Vittoria Carafa spent the evening and part of the night having these facts confirmed by all old Santi Quattro's friends. At seven o'clock the next morning she presented herself at the cardinal's home.

'Your Eminence,' she said to him, 'we are both of a certain age. It's pointless to try to delude each other by giving fine names to ugly things. I have come to present you with an absurd proposal. All I can say is that it is not harmful, but I must admit I find it truly ridiculous. When the matter of my daughter Elena's marriage to Ottavio Colonna arose, I took a liking to this young man and on the day of his marriage I will give you two hundred thousand piastres in lands or money, which I beg you to take to him. For a poor widow like me to make such a sacrifice I ask that my daughter Elena, now twenty-seven, who has not left the convent since she was nineteen, should be made abbess of Castro. For this to take place, by canon law, we must delay the election for six months.'

'What did you say, signora?' cried the outraged cardinal. 'His Holiness himself could not grant what you are now asking of a poor powerless old man.'

'That's why I told Your Eminence that the notion was ridiculous. Fools will think it mad, but experienced courtiers will think our excellent prince, Pope Gregory XIII, wanted to reward Your Eminence's long, loyal service by making possible a marriage all Rome knows you desire. As for the other thing, it is by no means out of the question. It's quite legal by church law; my daughter will take the white veil tomorrow.'

'But this is simony, signora,' cried the cardinal, outraged.

Signora de' Campireali turned to depart.

'What is this paper you are leaving here?'

'It's the list of lands valued at two hundred thousand piastres that I would give you unless you wanted it in silver. The change of title to these properties could be kept secret for a long time. Otherwise, the Colonna family could involve me in a trial that I might lose.'

'But it's simony, signora. Appalling simony.'

'First we must postpone the election for six months. Tomorrow I will come and take Your Eminence's orders.'

The next morning Vittoria Carafa learned that due to a serious mistake in the list of candidates for the position of abbess of Castro, the election was to be deferred for six months. The second nun on the list had a heretic in the family; one of her great-uncles had become a Protestant in Udine.

Signora de' Campireali decided she ought to make overtures to Prince Fabrizio Colonna, whose family she was about to offer such a noteworthy increase of income. After trying for two days, she managed to obtain an audience with him in a village near Rome. She left the audience in a state of panic. She had found the prince, usually such a calm person, so excited over the military prowess of Colonel Lizzara, that she judged it utterly pointless to ask him to keep the subject a secret. The colonel was a son to him and, more, a favoured pupil. The prince spent his time reading and rereading certain letters from Flanders.

What would become of the fine plan for which Signora de' Campireali had sacrificed so much for ten years if her daughter were to discover the true identity and glorious career of Colonel Lizzara?

Within two years of Signora de' Campireali's audience with Prince Colonna, Elena had been installed as Abbess of Castro, but Cardinal Santi Quattro had died of grief over this act of simony. The then Bishop of Castro, Francesco Cittadini, a Milanese nobleman, was the handsomest man in the pope's court. Noted for his modest charm and dignified bearing, he had many meetings with the Abbess of the Visitation, particularly over the matter of the new cloister with which she had decided to embellish the convent.

Young Bishop Cittadini, then twenty-nine, fell madly in love with the beautiful abbess. At the trial which ultimately took place, a throng of nuns called as witnesses reported that the bishop took the opportunity to visit the convent as often as he could, saying to the abbess, 'Elsewhere I command and I confess to my shame that I find pleasure in it. But before you I obey like a slave with a joy that far outweighs that of commanding anywhere else. I feel I am in the presence of a superior being, and, were I to try, I would have no other will but hers. I would rather be the lowliest of her slaves than a king out of her sight.'

The witnesses reported that even while he uttered these eloquent words the abbess would command him to be quiet in cutting terms that showed her contempt.

'To tell the truth,' another witness went on, 'the signora abbess treated him like a lackey, on which occasions the poor bishop would lower his eyes and begin to weep, but he would not leave. Every day he found new excuses to come to the convent. These visits deeply scandalized the nuns' confessors and the abbess's enemies. But the signora abbess was hotly defended by her close friend the prioress, who, under her direct command, exercised internal rule over the convent.'

'As you are aware, noble sisters,' the prioress said, 'ever since that perverse attraction for a soldier of fortune our abbess held in her young days, she has clung to many odd notions, but you all know this about her – she does not change her view of those to whom she has once shown contempt. She may never in her life have spoken so harshly to anyone as she has in front of us to poor Monsignor Cittadini. Every day we watch him cringe at the treatment that makes us blush for his high position.'

'Indeed,' replied the scandalized nuns, 'but he still comes back every day, therefore at heart he is not so badly treated, and, in any case, the apparent intrigue harms the reputation of the Holy Order of the Visitation.'

The harshest master would not have castigated his most feckless servant in the terms that the abbess used daily to the unctuous young bishop. But he was in love, and he brought from Milan the basic tenet that once a man has undertaken an enterprise of this nature he should concentrate on the goal and cease to concern himself with the means.

'In short,' said the bishop to his confidant Cesare del Bene, 'the lover who gives up his assault before he is confronted by superior strength is the one who incurs contempt.'

In November 1572, at eleven o'clock in the evening, the young bishop went alone to the church door, where by day the faithful were usually admitted. The abbess herself received him there and gave him leave to follow her. She took him to a room where she spent much of her time and from which a secret passage led to the galleries that overlooked the church nave. Barely an hour passed before the bewildered bishop was sent away. The abbess herself escorted him back to the church door.

'Goodbye, Monsignor,' she said. 'Leave me at once and return to your palazzo. I cannot abide you; I feel as if I had given myself to a lackey.'

Three months later Carnival came round. The people of Castro were well known for their festivities. The whole town resounded to the din of the procession. Everyone made a point of passing by a little window which afforded a glimpse into a certain stable in the convent. It was well known that three months before the Carnival this stable had been turned into a salon and on the days of the masked processions was always full of people.

In the midst of the general carousing the young bishop arrived in his carriage. The abbess gave him a sign, and that night at one o'clock he duly appeared at the church door. He entered, but less than three-quarters of an hour later he was angrily thrown out. Since their first meeting in November, he had turned up at the convent at least once a week. A little smirk of fatuous triumph could be seen on his face. This escaped no one, but it contrived to cast a pall upon the abbess's lofty character. On Easter Monday, among other days, she treated him like mere scum and spoke to him in terms that the lowliest convent scullion would not have borne. Yet a few days later she made a sign to him, and the handsome bishop presented himself at the church door at midnight. She had sent for him to say that she was with child.

At this news the young man blenched and fell dumb with horror. The abbess, becoming ill, sent for the doctor and made no secret of her condition. The man knew of his patient's generosity and promised to solve the problem for her. His first step was to put her in touch with a pretty young local woman who, while not a midwife, was practised in that art. Her husband was a baker. Elena was pleased with the woman's manner. The baker's wife said that to do what was necessary to help the abbess, she would need two accomplices in the convent.

'I can accept a woman like you when the time comes,' Elena told her, 'but not one of my equals. Now leave me alone.'

The midwife withdrew. But a few hours later, realizing it would be unwise to expose herself to the woman's gossip, Elena sent for the doctor, who made the midwife return to the convent, where she was generously rewarded. The woman swore that, even if not called back, she would never disclose the secret entrusted to her. Again she said that if within the convent there were not two women devoted to the abbess who could be told everything, she could not become involved. She feared being accused of infanticide.

After long thought, the abbess decided to confide the terrible secret to Donna Vittoria, the prioress, who was of a noble family, and to Donna Bernarda, the daughter of a marquis. She made them swear on their breviaries never to reveal a word, even before a penitentiary court, of what she was about to tell them. The women froze in terror. Later, under questioning, they swore that knowing the abbess's haughty spirit they expected a confession to a murder.

'I have failed in my duties,' the abbess said coldly and calmly, 'I am with child.'

Sorrowing and deeply moved owing to her long-standing friendship with Elena and in no way prompted by idle curiosity, the prioress asked tearfully, 'Who is the scoundrel who has committed this crime?'

'I have not revealed that even to my confessor,' said the abbess. 'Do you think I would tell you?'

The two women at once began to work out how to hide the deadly secret from the rest of the convent. They first decided that the abbess's bed should be moved from her present room to the pharmacy that had just been set up in the convent's furthest corner on the third storey of the wing endowed by Elena. There the abbess bore a male child. For three weeks the baker's wife had been hidden in the prioress's room. As the woman strode swiftly along the cloister, carrying the child, the baby began to cry. Terrified, the woman hid in the cellar. An hour later, with the help of the doctor, Donna Bernarda opened the garden door, and the baker's wife slipped out of the convent and thence out of the town. When she reached the open countryside she was siezed by a fit of panic and hid in a cave she found by chance among the rocks.

The abbess wrote to Cesare del Bene, the bishop's confidant and manservant, who rushed on horseback to the cave described to him, where he took the infant in his arms and galloped to Montefiascone. Baptised in the church of Santa Margherita, the child was given the name Alessandro. A landlady there found a wet nurse to whom Cesare gave eight scudi. A crowd of women gathered round the church during the baptismal ceremony, loudly asking Cesare the name of the child's father.

'He's a great Roman lord,' said he, 'who took advantage of a poor village woman like one of you.'

And he left.

VII

In the vast convent, with its three hundred inquisitive women, everything had gone well until then. No one had seen anything, no one had heard anything. But the abbess had given the doctor a few handfuls of newly minted *zecchini* of Roman coinage. He passed on several of these to the baker's wife. The woman was pretty, and her husband jealous. He rummaged in her coffer, found the gold pieces, and, supposing them the price of her shame, forced her at knife point to tell him how she'd come by them.

After some prevarication, the woman confessed the truth, and the couple made peace. They then pondered how to spend such a large sum. The baker's wife wanted to pay off some debts, but her husband thought it better to buy a mule, which was what they did. The mule caused a commotion in the neighbourhood as everyone knew that the couple were very poor. All the town gossips, friends and enemies, came in turn to ask the baker's wife who was the generous lover who had given her the wherewithal to buy a mule. Distressed, the woman admitted the truth.

One day when Cesare del Bene had been to see the child and was coming back to report on his visit to the abbess, she, although still very weak, dragged herself to the grille and accused him of being careless about the agents he had employed. The bishop, meanwhile, succumbed to fear. He wrote to his brothers in Milan to tell them of the false accusations being levelled against him, and he appealed to them to come to his aid. Although seriously ill, he chose to leave Castro, but before starting out he wrote to the abbess:

You must know by now that everything that happened is public knowledge. Therefore, if you have any interest in saving not only my reputation but perhaps my life, and to avoid a greater scandal, you might lay the blame on Giambattista Doleri, who died a few days ago. Even if in this way you cannot retrieve your own honour, mine at least will no longer be at risk.

The bishop sent for Don Luigi, the convent's confessor. 'Deliver this straight into the hands of the abbess,' he told him.

On reading the cowardly note, Elena cried out to everyone in the room, 'Thus do foolish virgins who put beauty of the body before that of the soul deserve to be treated.'

Rumours of all that was happening in Castro soon reached the ears of the fearsome Cardinal Farnese, who had been building up his reputation for several years in the hope of getting the vote of the most zealous cardinals at the next conclave. He immediately ordered the mayor of Castro to arrest Bishop Cittadini. Fearing interrogation, the bishop's entire household took flight. Only Cesare del Bene remained faithful to his master, swearing that he would die under torture rather than admit anything that could damage the bishop. Finding himself under close guard in his own palazzo, Cittadini again wrote to his brothers, and they hastened from Milan to find him detained in the Ronciglione prison.

At her first interrogation, while admitting her crime, the abbess denied having had relations with the bishop. Her paramour had been Giambattista Doleri, the convent's lawyer.

On 9 September 1575, Gregory XIII ordered that the trial proceed with all haste and the utmost rigour. A judge, a prosecutor, and a police superintendent made their way to Castro and Ronciglione. Cesare del Bene, the bishop's head manservant, admitted only having taken an infant to a wet nurse. He was interrogated in the presence of Donna Vittoria and Donna Bernarda. Tortured for two days, he endured frightful suffering, but true to his word he admitted only what it was impossible to deny. The prosecutor could drag no more out of him.

When the turns of Vittoria and Bernarda came, having witnessed the torture inflicted on Cesare, they confessed to everything they had done. All the nuns were questioned about the name of the criminal. Most replied that they had heard it said that it was the bishop. One of the gatekeeper nuns reported the offensive words that the abbess had used when showing the bishop out of the church.

'When people speak to each other in that tone, they have been lovers for a long time,' she added. 'Indeed, the Monsignor, whose conceit was usually noticeable for its excess, looked thoroughly sheepish as he left the church.'

One of the nuns, questioned before the instruments of torture, replied that the author of the crime must have been the cat, because it was always in the abbess's arms being lavishly fondled. Another nun claimed that the perpetrator of the crime must have been the wind, because on windy days the abbess was always happy and in a good mood. She would climb to the top of the bell tower she'd had constructed for this purpose and stand there in the teeth of the gale. When asked a favour in this spot, she never refused. The baker's wife, the wet nurse, and the gossips of Montefiascone, terrified by the tortures they'd seen inflicted on Cesare, spoke the truth.

The young bishop was ill, or pretending to be ill, in Ronciglione, and so his brothers, backed by Signora de' Campireali's wealth and influence, took the opportunity to throw themselves at the pope's feet, begging him to postpone the trial until the bishop had recovered his health. At this point Cardinal Farnese increased the number of guards on the bishop's prison. As the bishop could not be questioned, the prosecutors began all their sessions by putting the abbess to a fresh interrogation.

One day, after her mother had told her to be brave and go on denying everything, Elena admitted all.

'Why did you first blame Giambattista Doleri?'

'Out of pity for the cowardly bishop. Besides, if he manages to save his precious neck, he can provide for my son.'

After this admission, the abbess was locked in a room in the convent whose walls and vaulted ceiling were eight feet thick. This dungeon was known as the monk's room, and the nuns always spoke of it with terror. There three women kept watch over the abbess.

As the bishop's health began to improve, three hundred secret police and soldiers arrived at Ronciglione to escort him to Rome in a litter. There they confined him in the prison known as Corte Savella. A few days later the nuns were also brought to Rome. The abbess was placed in the Convent of Santa Marta. Four nuns were accused: Donna Vittoria and Donna Bernarda, the nun through whom messages were passed, and the gatekeeper who had overheard the insulting words the abbess had spoken to the bishop.

The bishop was questioned by the prosecutor, one of the leading members of the judiciary. Poor Cesare del Bene was once more tortured. Not only did he admit nothing but he also said things that annoyed the prosecuting magistrate, which resulted in another session of torture. Preliminary torture was also inflicted on Donna Vittoria and Donna Bernarda. The bishop denied everything with abusive language and great stubbornness. He gave a detailed account of all he had done on the three evenings he had clearly spent with the abbess.

Finally the abbess was brought face to face with the bishop and although she spoke nothing but the truth she was tortured. As she went on repeating what she had said since her initial statement, the bishop, true to the part he was playing, hurled insults at her.

After several other procedures, justifiable in themselves yet tainted with the spirit of cruelty that, following the reigns of Charles V and Philip II, too often prevailed in Italian courts, the bishop was sentenced to life imprisonment in the Castel Sant' Angelo. The abbess was condemned to be detained for life in the Convent of Santa Marta. But Signora de' Campireali had already begun to have an underground tunnel dug. This tunnel started in one of the sewers dating from the days of ancient Rome and was to emerge in the deep cellar where the mortal remains of the nuns of Santa Marta were deposited.

The two-foot-wide tunnel was shored up, and as the workmen advanced they roofed the excavation with pairs of planks set in the form of a capital A.

This passageway lay about thirty feet below ground. The main problem was to aim it in the right direction. All along the way, the men had to swerve round wells and the foundations of ancient buildings. Another great problem was the rubble, which they were hard put to dispose of. Apparently they sprinkled it by night along the Roman streets. Everyone was amazed by all this soil that seemed to have fallen from the sky.

No matter how much money Signora de' Campireali might spend in trying to rescue her daughter, the underground passage would undoubtedly have been discovered had Pope Gregory XIII not died in 1585, after which an era of chaos reigned while the papal throne remained vacant.

In Santa Marta Elena was badly treated. We can easily imagine how the simple, impoverished nuns were only too prepared to make a misery of the life of a rich abbess convicted of such a crime. Elena was impatiently awaiting the results of her mother's earthworks, when all at once her feelings changed. Six months earlier, noting the pope's fragile state of health and having great plans for the interregnum, Fabrizio Colonna had sent one of his officers to Giulio Branciforte, now well known in the Spanish army under the name of Colonel Lizzara. The prince ordered him back to Italy, and Giulio yearned to see his native land again. Under an assumed name he landed at Pescara, a small Adriatic port near Chieti in the Abruzzi, and journeyed over the mountains to La Petrella. The prince's joy astonished everyone.

He told Giulio he had sent for him to make him his successor and commander of his troops. To which Branciforte replied that, speaking as a soldier, he believed the prince's plan was doomed to failure, as he quickly demonstrated. Within six months and at little cost, Spain, if she so desired, could put paid to all the soldiers of fortune in Italy.

'However, sire,' added young Branciforte, 'if you wish, I am ready to march. You will always find in me a worthy successor to our late Ranuccio.'

Before Giulio's arrival, the prince in his customary manner had ordered that no one in La Petrella should speak of Castro or of the abbess's trial. Death without appeal would be the penalty for the slightest careless word. In the midst of joyous celebrations to welcome Branciforte, the prince told him never to go to Albano on his own. To make the journey possible, Colonna billeted a thousand of his men in the town and sent an advance party of twelve hundred men along the road to Rome. We can imagine poor Giulio's feelings when the prince had old Scotti brought to the house that he had made his head-quarters and welcomed him into the room where he and Branciforte were sitting.

Once the two friends had thrown themselves into each other's arms, the prince said to Giulio, 'Now, my poor Colonel, prepare for the worst.'

At this he blew out the candle and left, locking the two men in.

The next day, not wishing to leave his room, Giulio sent to ask the prince's permission to return to La Petrella but not to see him for a few days. However, he was informed that the prince had left, together with his troops. During the night, hearing of Gregory XIII's death, the prince had forgotten his friend Giulio and was rushing about the countryside. In those days, while the throne was vacant, the law was silent. Each man set out to satisfy his passions, and the only law was that of violence. This was how, before the end of the day, Prince Colonna had had fifty of his enemies hanged. Thirty men of Ranuccio's original company remained with Giulio. Accompanied by this small troop, he took the step of marching to Rome.

All the Abbess of Castro's servants had remained faithful to her. They were lodging in tumbledown houses near the Convent of Santa Marta. Gregory XIII's final illness had lasted more than a week. Before attacking the last fifty yards of her tunnel, Signora de' Campiriali waited impatiently for the lawless days that were to follow the pope's death. As the passage had to cut through the cellars of several inhabited houses, she was afraid she might not be able to keep the final stretch hidden from public view.

Two days after Branciforte's arrival at La Petrella, the three of Giulio's former *bravi* whom Elena had taken into her service seemed to become touched by madness. Although everyone knew that the abbess was in total seclusion and guarded by nuns who hated her, Ugone, one of the *bravi*, came to the gate of Santa Marta and insisted on being allowed to see his mistress at once. He was stopped and thrown out. In despair, he took up a stance at the gate and set about distributing *baiocchi* to the convent's servants, who were coming and going, and telling them, 'Rejoice with me. Signor Giulio Branciforte is back. Tell all your friends he's alive.'

Ugone's two companions spent the day bringing him fresh supplies of *baiocchi*, which they handed out night and day, repeating the same words, until they hadn't a single coin left. But the three *bravi* continued to take turns at the door of the Convent of Santa Marta, still addressing everyone who passed with the eager words, 'Signor Giulio has returned.'

Their plan succeeded. Less than thirty-six hours after the first coin had been distributed, poor Elena in the depths of her hidden dungeon knew that Giulio was alive. The word threw her into a frenzy.

'Oh, my mother,' she cried out, 'haven't you harmed me enough?'

A few hours later, the amazing news was confirmed by little Marietta, who, by sacrificing all her golden jewellery, had obtained leave to follow the nun whose turn it was to bring the prisoner her meals. With tears of joy, Elena threw herself into the girl's arms.

'This is indeed good news,' said Elena, 'but I will not be with you much longer.'

'Of course you will,' said Marietta. 'I don't believe that the period of the conclave will pass without your prison being changed to simple exile.'

'Oh, my dear, to see Giulio again! And to see him with this guilt on my head!'

In the middle of the third night following this conversation, part of the church's stone floor caved in with a loud crash. The nuns thought that the convent was about to collapse. Everyone believed there had been an earthquake, and chaos ensued. An hour or so later, preceded by the three *bravi* in Elena's service, Signora de' Campireali reached the dungeon through the underground passage.

'Success, signora, success!' cried the *bravi*.

Elena was frightened to death. She thought Giulio Branciforte was with them. They calmed her, and her face resumed its stony expression when they told her that only Signora de' Campireali was with them. Giulio was in Albano, which he had just occupied with several thousand soldiers.

After a moment or two, Signora de' Campireali appeared. Walking with some difficulty, she leaned on the arm of her equerry, who was in full dress, sword at his side. His sumptuous clothes were soiled with mud.

'My dearest Elena, I've come to rescue you!' cried her mother.

'Who told you that I wanted to be rescued?'

Signora de' Campireali was astounded. She gazed

wide-eyed at her daughter, who appeared deeply disturbed.

'My dear Elena,' she said at last, 'events force me to admit to an act that was perhaps understandable after all the misfortunes that befell our family but of which I now repent and beg your forgiveness. Giulio Branciforte is alive.'

'Precisely because he is alive I no longer wish to live.'

At first Signora de' Campireali could not fathom what her daughter was saying and begged her to explain, but to no avail. Having turned to her crucifix, Elena had ceased listening and was praying. Vainly, for a whole hour, Signora de' Campireali did her utmost to elicit a word or a look.

At last her daughter said impatiently, 'It was under the marble base of this crucifix in my little room at Albano that his letters were hidden. You should have let my father stab me to death! Go, and leave me some gold.'

Again Signora de' Campireali tried to speak to her daughter in spite of the frantic signals that her equerry was making to her. Elena lost patience.

'Allow me at least an hour of freedom,' she said. 'You have poisoned my life, now you want to poison my death as well.'

'We can hold the underground tunnel for another two or three hours. I dare hope you will change your mind!' said Signora de' Campireali, bursting into tears.

And she withdrew down the tunnel.

'Ugone, stay with me,' Elena said. 'Look to your weapons, my friend, for you may need to protect me. Let's see your dirk, your rapier, your dagger.'

The old soldier showed her these weapons, all in perfect condition.

'Good, now wait outside my cell. I'm going to write Giulio a long letter which you will take to him yourself. As I have nothing with which to seal it, I do not want it to go by hands other than yours. Put in your pockets all the gold my mother left. I need only fifty *zecchini* for myself. Lay them on my bed.'

After she had spoken, Elena began to write.

You have my complete trust, dear Giulio. If I take my leave, it is because I would die of remorse in your arms, glimpsing what my happiness could have been had I not committed a sin. Never believe I ever loved any being on earth after you. On the contrary, my heart has nothing but the deepest contempt for the man I let into my room. My offence was merely boredom, and, if you like, wantonness. Remember that my spirit was weakened after the useless journey I made to La Petrella, where the prince I revered, because you loved him, received me so cruelly. Remember, I say to you, that I was worn down by twelve years of falsehood. Everything around me was falsehood and lies and I knew it. At the start I received some thirty letters from you. Imagine the joy with which I opened the first ones. But as I read, my heart grew cold. I looked carefully at the writing, I recognised your hand but not your heart. This initial lie poisoned the essence of my life such that I opened any subsequent letter in your writing without joy. The hideous news of your death contrived to kill off all that remained of the happy times when we were young. As you will understand, my first plan was to go and see and touch with my hand the Mexican shore where it was said that savages had murdered you. If only I had carried out this plan we would now be happy, for in Madrid, however many spies a watchful hand had sown around me, since I myself would have aroused the pity of all the hearts in which there remained an ounce of mercy or good will, I would probably have discovered the truth. For, my Giulio, your brave deeds had already attracted the notice of the world, and perhaps someone in Madrid knew you were Branciforte. Shall I tell you what stood in the way of our happiness? First, the memory of the cruel, humiliating reception that the prince gave me at La Petrella. From Castro to Mexico, what a powerful obstacle to surmount! You see, my soul had already lost its strength. I then began to indulge my vanity and had some large buildings erected in the convent. I wanted to be able to use as my room the porter's lodge, where you took refuge on the night of the battle. One day, as I was looking out on the soil where you had spilt your blood for me, I heard a word of abuse and, lifting my gaze, saw spiteful faces. To avenge myself, I decided to become abbess of this convent. My mother, who knew very well that you were alive, made heroic efforts to get me the outrageous nomination. The position has been nothing but a source of tedium to me. It has depraved my soul. I often took pleasure in displaying my power through the misfortunes of others. I committed unjust acts. At the age of thirty I found myself chaste according to the outside world, wealthy, influential, and yet utterly wretched. Then this poor man turned up, who, while the soul of goodness, was stupidity itself. It was owing to his foolishness that I fell in with his first approaches. My spirit was so worn down by everything round me since you left that it no longer had the strength to resist the smallest temptation. Shall I tell you something very shocking? Yes, I shall, for it seems to me that everything is allowed the dead. By the time you read these lines, worms will be devouring this vaunted beauty of mine that should have been for you alone. Finally, I must speak of what causes me most pain. I do not know why I did not play at casual love affairs like all our Roman ladies. I did have some licentious thoughts, but I was never able to give myself to that man without feeling horror and disgust, which cancelled out all the pleasure. I kept seeing you beside me in the garden of our palazzo in Albano, when the Madonna inspired in you that act which was generously intended but which my mother has used to destroy our lives. You were never threatening but remained as good and tender as ever. Then you looked at me. In a fit of rage at that other man I went so far as to hit him as hard as I could. This is the whole truth, dearest Giulio. I did not want to die without telling it to you, and I also thought that writing this letter would take away my wish to die. More than ever, I now realize had I kept myself worthy of you how happy I would be to see you again. I order you to live and continue in your military career, which gave me so much joy on hearing of your successes. What might have happened, great God, had I received your letters, particularly after the battle of Achêne! Live and think often of Ranuccio, killed at Ciampi, and of Elena, who, so as not to see the reproach in your eyes, lies dead at Santa Marta.

When she had finished writing, Elena went to the old soldier, who had fallen asleep. Unnoticed, she took his dagger and then woke him.

'I've finished,' she said. 'I fear our enemies may seize the underground passage. Go quickly, take my letter which is on the table, and deliver it to Giulio by your own hand – *by your own hand* – do you understand? Also, give him this handkerchief of mine. Tell him I love him as much at this moment as I always have – *always*, do you hear!'

Ugone was on his feet but he did not move.

'Go now!'

'Signora, have you really thought this over? Signor Giulio loves you so much.'

'I love him too. Put this letter into his hands.'

'Very well, and may God bless you for your goodness.'

Ugone left but quickly returned. Elena lay dead, his dagger in her heart.

VITTORIA ACCORAMBONI
Duchess of Bracciano

I

Unfortunately for me, as for the reader, this is not a work of fiction but a faithful translation of a sombre record set down in Padua in December 1585.

A few years ago I was in Mantua on the lookout for sketches and small pictures within my means, but I wanted paintings that dated from before 1600. It was about then that originality in Italian art, on the wane since the sacking of Florence, in 1530, finally petered out.

An extremely rich, miserly old aristocrat offered to sell me for a considerable price not pictures but some old manuscripts yellowed with age. I asked if I might look them over. He agreed, adding that he was relying on my honesty if I did not buy the manuscripts not to remember any of the spicy stories I might read in them.

On this understanding, which appealed to me – but to the great detriment of my eyes – I made my way through three or four hundred volumes in which, two or three centuries earlier, accounts of tragic events, challenges to duels, peace treaties between neighbouring noble families, and memoirs on every kind of subject had been hoarded. The elderly owner was asking a high price for the lot. After a good deal of negotiation I contrived to buy at some cost the right to make copies of certain short tales that I liked and that illustrate Italian customs going back to the year 1500. I have twenty-two folio volumes of them, and it is one of these faithfully translated stories that I now offer to the reader – that is, if he is gifted with patience. I am familiar with sixteenth-century Italian history and I believe that what follows is perfectly true. I have taken care that the translation of this old Italian style, which is serious, direct, sinister, and full of allusions to events and ideas which preoccupied the world during the reign of Sixtus V (1585), should contain no resonances of modern writing nor any ideas from our own unprejudiced century.

The anonymous author of this manuscript is a cautious individual; he offers no opinions nor does he rearrange facts in any way. His sole concern is to tell the story accurately. If he is sometimes unwittingly graphic it is because, in 1585, vanity did not surround every act with a halo of affectation. It was believed that one person could only influence another by explaining himself as clearly as possible. With the exception of courtiers and poets, no one in 1585 would have said, 'I will die at Your Majesty's feet', when he had just sent for post horses to make his escape. This particular form of treachery was not yet invented. People then spoke little, and each paid great attention to what was said to him.

Therefore, kind reader, do not search in these pages for a striking style, shimmering with fresh allusions to fashionable modes of thought. Above all, do not expect the cloying emotions of a George Sand novel. That great writer would have created a masterpiece out of the life and misfortunes of Vittoria Accoramboni. The version I present to you can only make the more modest claims of history. When, by chance, in haste alone, at nightfall, our thoughts turn to the great art of understanding the human heart, we might well heed the historical incidents related here. The author reports everything, explains everything, leaves nothing to the reader's imagination. He was writing twelve days after the heroine's death.

II

Vittoria Accoramboni was born to one of the noblest of families in a little town called Gubbio, in the Duchy of Urbino. Since childhood she had been noted for her arresting beauty. But beauty was the least of her charms. She lacked no quality among those which inspire admiration in a girl of high birth. But there was nothing, you might say, so particularly remarkable about her, nothing which stood out among her exceptional qualities so much as a certain enchanting grace, which captured the hearts and good will of everyone. This candour, which endowed her slightest utterance with authority, was unmarred by the least trace of artifice. Had you no more than set eyes on her it would have taken all your strength to resist her charms. But once you heard her speak, especially if you held a conversation with her, it was quite impossible to escape her extraordinary allure.

Many of the young noblemen in Rome, where her father lived and where his palazzo still stands in the Piazza Rusticucci, near St Peter's, aspired to her hand. There was much jealousy and plenty of rivalry, but eventually Vittoria's parents chose Felice Peretti, a nephew of Cardinal Montalto, who by God's grace now reigns as Pope Sixtus V.

The son of Camilla Peretti, the cardinal's sister, Felice's original name was Francesco Mignucci. He took the name Felice Peretti when his uncle formally adopted him.

Vittoria's natural superiority, which could be called disastrous and which she unwittingly exuded wherever she went, accompanied her when she entered the Peretti household. Her husband's love for her fell little short of madness. Her mother-in-law Camilla and Cardinal Montalto himself seemed to have no other occupation than to discover and satisfy Vittoria's least wish. All Rome watched with fascination to see how the cardinal, who was as well known for his scant means as for his horror of all forms of extravagance, found unending pleasure in anticipating Vittoria's every wish. Young, beautiful, adored by all, she was often prey to costly fancies. From her new parents Vittoria received the most expensive jewellery, pearls, and in due course whatever seemed rarest at the Roman goldsmiths, so sumptuously stocked in those days.

For love of this dear niece, Cardinal Montalto, despite his famed harshness, treated Vittoria's brothers as if they had been his own nephews. At his intercession, Ottavio Accoramboni, then scarcely thirty years old, was nominated Bishop of Fossombrone by the Duke of Urbino and thus appointed by Pope

Gregory XIII. Marcello Accoramboni, a young man of fierce courage, accused of several crimes and hotly pursued by the Roman police, had with considerable difficulty evaded the pursuit which could have led to his death. Under the cardinal's protection, he was able to enjoy a certain respite.

Vittoria's third brother, Giulio Accoramboni – as soon as Cardinal Montalto made the request – was admitted by Cardinal Alessandro Sforza to the highest honours at his court.

In a word, if people could only measure happiness not by the endless insatiability of their desires but by the real enjoyment of advantages they already possess, Vittoria's marriage to Cardinal Montalto's nephew would have seemed to the Accoramboni the crowning happiness of life. But the senseless craving for vast but uncertain profit can drive those human beings most endowed with fortune's favours into strange and perilous undertakings.

Indeed, if some of Vittoria's relatives – as many people in Rome suspected – helped to part her from her husband through their longing to amass a huge fortune, one might contend that they would have been wiser to have satisfied themselves with the modest advantages of a comfortable sum of money, which undoubtedly would soon have reached the pinnacle of all that ambition could desire.

While Vittoria was living in this way, a queen in her home, one night after Felice Peretti and his wife had retired to bed, a letter was given to him by a certain Caterina, Vittoria's Bologna-born maid. The letter had been delivered by one of Caterina's brothers, Domenico d'Aquaviva, nicknamed Mancino, for he was left-handed. This man had been banished from Rome for several crimes, but at Caterina's intercession Felice had obtained for him his uncle the cardinal's powerful protection. Mancino often came to Felice's house, for Felice trusted him implicitly.

The letter we are referring to was signed by Marcello Accoramboni, who of all Vittoria's brothers was the dearest to her husband. Most of the time Marcello lived in hiding outside Rome, but occasionally he risked entering the city, where he took refuge in Felice's house.

In the letter, delivered at such an unusually late hour, Marcello called on his brother-in-law for help. He begged Felice to come to his aid on a matter of the most pressing urgency, adding that he would wait near the Palazzo Montecavallo.

Felice showed his wife this strange letter, then he dressed and armed himself only with his rapier. Accompanied by a single servant, who carried a lighted torch, he was about to leave when his way was barred by his mother Camilla and all the women in the household, including Vittoria herself. They implored him not to go out at this late hour. As he paid no heed to their entreaties, they fell to their knees and with tears in their eyes begged him to listen to them.

These women, and particularly Camilla, had been horror-struck by the account of strange events which were happening daily and which went unpunished during the reign of Gregory XIII, a period beset by troubles and appalling crimes. One further fact struck them. When Marcello Accoramboni took the risk of coming to Rome, he never summoned Felice in this way, and such a step at this time of night seemed to them wholly unreasonable.

Primed with the heat of youth, Felice set no store by reasoning based on fear, and when he found out that the letter had been brought by Mancino, a man of whom he was extremely fond and to whom he had rendered services, nothing would stop him from leaving the house.

As we have said, a single servant went before him carrying a lighted brand, but poor young Felice had hardly taken a few steps up the slope of Montecavallo when he was felled by three shots from an arquebus. The murderers, seeing him on the ground, threw themselves on him and stabbed him repeatedly, until they were satisfied he was dead. This fateful news was at once carried to Felice's mother and wife and by them to his uncle the cardinal.

Without change of expression, without betraying his feelings in any degree, the cardinal quickly dressed and commended to God both his soul and that of the poor young man so unexpectedly taken. He then went to his niece's apartments, where, with admirable gravity and an air of deep serenity, he put a stop to the weeping and lamentation of the women, which had begun to resound through the house. Such was his authority over the women that from that moment, even when the corpse was carried out of the house, nothing was seen nor heard from any of them that diverged in the slightest from the behaviour of the best-regulated families at the most widely expected death. As for Cardinal Montalto, no one could catch a glimpse in him of even the mildest sign of ordinary grief. Nothing changed in the disposition or the outward appearance of his life. Rome, which with its usual curiosity watched every action performed by this deeply injured man, was soon baffled.

By chance the consistory was convoked at the Vatican on the day after Felice's violent death. Everyone in the city assumed that on the first day at least Cardinal Montalto would avoid this public function. There he would have to appear before a horde of inquisitive onlookers. They would note any sign of that natural weakness so essential for an eminent person to hide when he aspires to even greater eminence. For everyone knows that it is inappropriate for someone who hopes to raise himself above all others to show that he is the same as them.

But those who thought this way were doubly mistaken for, to begin with, as was his wont, Cardinal Montalto was among the first to enter the consistorial chamber, and, secondly, not even the most observant could detect in him any sign whatever of human emotion. On the contrary, by his response to those of his colleagues who, after such a brutal event, offered words of consolation he managed to confound everyone. His steadfastness and apparent rigidity in the face of such appalling misfortune at once became the talk of the town.

It is quite true that certain members of the consistory who were more experienced in court behaviour attributed this apparent coldness not to lack of feeling but to considerable dissimulation. This view was soon shared by most of the courtiers, for it was important not to seem too deeply wounded by a crime whose author was powerful and who might later block one's path to the highest office.

Whatever the reason for this seeming callousness, one thing is certain. Rome and the whole Papal Court were struck dumb. As for the consistory, after the cardinals had assembled, when the pope himself came into the chamber he instantly turned to Cardinal Montalto, and His Holiness's eyes filled with tears. But the cardinal's features did not stray from their usual impassivity.

The astonishment increased when Cardinal Montalto took his turn to kneel before His Holiness to give an account of matters in his care, and the pope, before allowing him to begin, could not hold back a sob. When His Holiness was able to speak, he tried to console the cardinal, promising him that instant justice would be meted out for such a fearful crime. But the cardinal, having humbly thanked His Holiness, begged him not to open an investigation into what had happened, protesting that he himself with all his heart forgave the perpetrator, whoever he might be. After this brief plea, the cardinal passed on to an account of normal business as if nothing unusual had taken place.

The gaze of every cardinal present was riveted on the pope and Montalto, and, although it is difficult to pull the wool over the experienced eyes of the court, no one dared say that Montalto's face betrayed the slightest emotion on seeing close up His Holiness reduced to tears. Cardinal Montalto's astonishing impassivity did not relax at all during the whole time that he worked with His Holiness. It was so noticeable that the pope himself was struck by it, and when the consistory had convened he could not help remarking to Cardinal San Sisto, his favourite nephew, '*Veramente, costui è un gran frate!*' In truth, this man is an arrogant friar.*

Cardinal Montalto's behaviour did not change in any way over the following days. As was the custom, he received consolatory visits from cardinals, prelates, and Roman princes, but, however close his friendship

---

* An allusion to the hypocrisy which nasty-minded people attributed to friars. Sixtus V had been a mendicant friar and persecuted within his order. See his life by Gregorio Leti, an amusing historian who was no greater liar than any of them.

with any of them, to none did he allow himself to utter a single word of grief or mourning. With everyone, after a short discussion on the unpredictability of human affairs, bolstered and corroborated by quotations from the Holy Scriptures or early Fathers, he instantly changed the subject and brought the conversation round to local news or personal matters concerning whomever he was with, just as if he wished to console his comforters.

Rome was especially interested in what would transpire at the visit that Prince Paolo Giordano Orsini, Duke of Bracciano, had been ordered to make, for gossip held him responsible for Felice Peretti's death. The common folk did not believe that Cardinal Montalto could find himself in intimate conversation with the prince without revealing some sign of his feelings.

When the prince arrived there was a huge crowd in the road outside the cardinal's door. Everyone was so eager to study the faces of the two speakers that the whole palazzo brimmed with courtiers. But no one saw anything unusual in either the one or the other. Cardinal Montalto behaved exactly according to court propriety. His face took on a noticeably jovial expression, and he spoke to the prince in an extremely affable manner.

A moment later, climbing back into his carriage and finding himself alone with courtiers who were his close friends, Prince Paolo blurted out with a laugh, '*In fatto, è vero che costui è un gran frate!*' By Jove, this man is in indeed an arrogant friar! It was as if he wished to confirm the truth of what the pope had let slip a few days earlier.

Wise heads considered that the conduct Cardinal Montalto had displayed cleared his way to the throne, for many shared his view that neither by nature or by force could he or would he harm whoever had committed the crime, although he had great reason to be distressed.

Felice Peretti had left nothing in writing concerning his wife. Consequently, she had to return to her parents. Before her departure, Cardinal Montalto gave her all the clothes, jewels, and in sum all the gifts she had received as his nephew's wife.

On the third day after Felice Peretti's death, Vittoria, together with her mother, installed herself in Prince Orsini's palazzo. It was said by some that the women were driven to this step by fear for their personal safety. The Curia appeared to threaten them with the accusation of being accessories to the murder – or at least with having had prior knowledge of it. Others thought (and what happened later seemed to bear this out) that they were led to this measure in order to bring about a marriage, since the prince had promised to marry Vittoria as soon as she no longer had a husband.

Nevertheless, neither then nor later was anyone sure who was responsible for Felice's death, although everyone suspected everyone else. Most, however, blamed Prince Orsini. It was widely known that he had been in love with Vittoria. He had given unmistakable indications, and the marriage which came about was clear proof, for the woman was of such inferior social standing that only the tyranny of passion could elevate her to matrimonial equality. The common people were in no way dissuaded from this view by a letter sent to the governor of Rome only a few days afterwards. It was signed by Cesare Palantieri, a young man of stormy character who had been banished from the city.

In his letter Palantieri said that there was no need for His Most Illustrious Excellency to trouble himself with looking elsewhere for the author of Felice Peretti's death, because he himself had had him killed following a disagreement that had taken place between them some time before.

Few believed that the murder could have been committed without the consent of the Accoramboni family. They blamed Vittoria's brothers, who had been drawn by ambition into an alliance with a rich and powerful prince. Marcello, in particular, was accused on account of the letter that had prompted the unfortunate Felice to leave his home. Vittoria herself was maligned when they saw her so soon after her husband's death agreeing to live in the Palazzo Orsini as a future wife. People claimed that it was hardly likely that a man would be able to use small arms in the wink of an eye if he had been handling long-range weapons for some time.

On the orders of Gregory XIII, the murder investigation was undertaken by Monsignor Portici, the governor of Rome. The only evidence was that of Domenico, nicknamed Mancino, arrested by the Curia, who confessed without being put to the torture on 24 February 1582 during his second interrogation, that 'Vittoria's mother was the cause of it all, and she was aided and abetted by the maidservant from Bologna, who, immediately after the murder, took refuge in the fortress of Bracciano, belonging to Prince Orsini, and where the *corte* dared not enter; and that the assassins were Marchione di Gubbio and Paolo Barca da Bracciano, tried and trusty knights of a lord whose name, for valid reasons, could not be revealed.'

In my view, these valid reasons supplemented the earnest request of Cardinal Montalto, who was insistent that investigations should be taken no further and that, in sum, there should be no question of a trial. Mancino was released from prison and formally warned under pain of death to return directly to his country and never to leave it without express permission. He was freed on Santa Lucia's day in 1583, and the fact that this was also Cardinal Montalto's birthday more and more confirms my belief that it was at his request the matter was closed. Under a government as weak as that of Gregory XIII, such a trial could have had most disagreeable consequences to no purpose at all.

The activities of the Curia thus came to an end, but Pope Gregory XIII had no intention of agreeing to a marriage between Prince Paolo Orsini, Duke of Bracciano, and the widow Accoramboni. Having condemned the latter to a sort of prison sentence, His Holiness issued a warning to the prince and the widow not to arrange a marriage contract without his express permission or that of his successors.

When Gregory XIII died at the beginning of 1585 and the lawyers consulted by Prince Paolo Orsini concluded that the pope's warning was nullified by the death of the person who had imposed it, the prince resolved to marry Vittoria before a new pope was elected. But the marriage could not take place as early as the prince wished, partly because he wanted the consent of Vittoria's brothers – and it so happened that Ottavio Accoramboni, Bishop of Fossombrone, refused ever to give his – and partly because nobody believed that the election of Gregory XIII's successor would occur immediately. The fact is that the wedding took place on the very day that Cardinal Montalto, who was so closely concerned in the matter, was made pope – that is, on 24 April 1585. Either this was sheer coincidence or the prince was determined to show that he did not fear the Curia under the new pope any more than he had done under Gregory XIII.

The marriage deeply offended Sixtus V, for this

was the name chosen by Cardinal Montalto. He had already abandoned the kind of thinking appropriate to a monk and had raised his soul to the heights of the position to which God had just elevated him.

The pope, however, showed no sign of anger. But as Prince Orsini presented himself that very day along with the mass of Roman lords to kiss the pope's foot (his secret aim was to try to determine from the Holy Father's expression what to expect or fear from this man, who until now was so little known), he realized that the time for levity was over. The new pope regarded him with a strange expression and, as His Holiness made no reply to the compliment addressed him by the prince, Orsini resolved to find out there and then the pope's intentions regarding him.

Through Ferdinando, Cardinal de' Medici – the brother of the prince's first wife – and also through the Catholic ambassador, Orsini requested and obtained an audience with the pope in his chambers. There, in a prepared speech, he addressed His Holiness, and, making no mention of the past, he rejoiced with the pope on the occasion of his new office and pledged him, as faithful vassal and servant, all his property and all his strength.

The pope listened carefully, and, when the prince had finished, replied that no one desired more than he that the life and deeds of Paolo Giordano Orsini should in the future be worthy of the Orsini blood

and of a true Christian knight; that, as for his conduct in the past towards the Holy See and towards
the person of the pope himself, no one would be
better able to address him on this than his own
conscience; that, meanwhile, the prince should
understand one thing, which was that although His
Holiness willingly forgave Orsini for what he might
have done against Felice Peretti and against Felice
Cardinal Montalto, he would never forgive what in
the future he might do against Pope Sixtus; that,
consequently, the pope would prevail upon him to
go at once and expel from his household and from
his estates all the brigands and criminals to whom, at
present, he was giving refuge.

Sixtus V was always remarkably effective in whatever
tone of voice he adopted, but when he was angered
and threatening it could be said that lightning
flashed from his eyes. What is certain is that Prince
Paolo Orsini, who was accustomed to holding popes
in awe, was forced by the pope's manner of speaking
to think more seriously about his affairs than he had
done in the past thirteen years. Accordingly, as soon
as he left His Holiness's palazzo, he rushed to Cardinal
de' Medici to tell him what had just taken place. On
the cardinal's advice, the prince resolved to banish
immediately all those outlaws whom he was harbouring
in his palazzo and estates, and he made haste to think
up a reasonable pretext for leaving any lands under
the sway of such a determined pontiff.

It should be realized that Paolo Orsini had grown enormously fat. His legs were thicker than a normal man's body, and one of these massive limbs was infected with a disease called *la lupa*, the she wolf, named thus because it had to be fed with large amounts of fresh meat, which were applied to the infected area. Otherwise, the raging disease, not finding dead flesh to devour, would hurl itself upon the living flesh which surrounded it.

The prince hit on the excuse of this affliction to visit the famous baths at Abano, near Padua, a dependency of the Venetian Republic. He left with his new wife around the middle of June. Abano was a very safe place for him, because for many years the house of Orsini had been allied to the Venetian Republic through mutual services.

Once he arrived in this safe haven, the prince thought only of enjoying the delights of several sojourns, and, with this plan in mind, he rented three splendid palazzi, one in Venice, the Palazzo Dandoli, in the Rio della Zecca; the second, the Palazzo Foscarini, in Padua, in the magnificent Piazza l'Arena; and a third, in Salò, on the beautiful shores of Lake Garda, in the palazzo that once belonged to the Sforza Pallavicini.

The Venetian nobles, who governed the Republic, were delighted to learn of the arrival in their land of such a great prince, and at once they offered him a generous contract as a condottiere – that is to say, a large annual sum, which was to be used by the prince to levy a body of two or three thousand mercenaries who would be under his command. The prince quickly declined the offer. He sent a reply to the senators saying that although by natural inclination and family tradition he felt deeply devoted to the Most Serene Republic, nevertheless, as he was at present attached to the Catholic king, he did not think it proper to accept another engagement. Such a determined reply somewhat cooled the senators' enthusiasm. On his arrival in Venice they had originally intended in the name of the people to organize an elaborate reception. Following the prince's reply, they decided to let him make his appearance as a private individual.

On being informed of this, Prince Orsini decided not even to go to Venice. By then nearing Padua, he made a diversion into that beautiful countryside and appeared with his entire household at the house prepared for him on the shores of Lake Garda. He spent the whole summer there enjoying the most pleasant and varied pastimes.

The season to move on came round, and the prince undertook a few small excursions, following which he seemed less able than before to stand the strain. Fearing for his health, he considered spending a few days in Venice, but he was dissuaded from this by his wife Vittoria, who made him stay on in Salò.

Some people think that Vittoria Accoramboni

was aware of the danger which daily surrounded the prince her husband and that she only persuaded him to stay in Salò because she intended later to leave Italy and take him, perhaps, to some free town in Switzerland. In this way, in the event of the prince's death, she would safeguard herself and her personal fortune.

Whether there was any truth in this hypothesis, the fact is that nothing of the sort took place, for on 10 November, afflicted by a new malady, the prince had a premonition of what was about to happen.

He took pity on his unfortunate wife. He foresaw her in the full bloom of youth as poor in reputation as in possessions, loathed by the reigning princes of Italy, little loved by the Orsini, and with no hope of another marriage after his death. A generous man, of loyal faith, he drew up a will by his own hand in which he tried to secure the property of the unfortunate lady. He bequeathed to her the sum of a hundred thousand scudi in money and jewels, and all the horses, carriages, and effects which he had used during the journey. The rest of his estate he left to Virginio Orsini, his only son by his first wife, the sister of Grand Duke Francesco I of Tuscany, whom he'd had killed with her brother's consent for unfaithfulness.

But even a man's best laid plans are never certain. The arrangements Paolo Orsini had thought would guarantee the poor young woman's complete security led her to ruin and destruction.

After signing his will on 12 November, the prince

felt a little better. On the morning of the 13th he was bled, and the doctors, pinning their hopes on a strict diet, left clear orders that he eat nothing.

But they had barely left the room when the prince demanded that dinner be served him. No one dared disobey, and he ate and drank as usual. No sooner had he finished the meal than he lost consciousness and two hours before sunset he was dead.

After this sudden demise, accompanied by her brother Marcello and the dead prince's whole court, Vittoria Accoramboni left for Padua to the Palazzo Foscarini, the palace that the prince had rented.

Shortly after her arrival she was joined by her brother Flaminio, who enjoyed the patronage of Cardinal Farnese. Vittoria began to undertake the necessary steps to obtain payment of the legacy that her husband had left her. This legacy amounted to sixty thousand scudi, which were to be paid to her over a period of two years. The sum was independent of her dowry, jointure, and all the jewels and furniture already in her possession. Prince Orsini had laid down in his will that in Rome, or in any other town of the duchess's choice, a palazzo should be purchased for her to the value of ten thousand scudi and a country house to the value of six thousand. He had also stipulated that her table and household should be equipped as befitted a woman of her rank. The household should consist of forty servants, with a corresponding number of horses.

Signora Vittoria placed considerable hopes on the help of the princes of Ferrara, Florence, and Urbino, and on that of cardinals Farnese and de' Medici, named executors of his will by the deceased prince. It should be noted that the will had been drawn up in Padua and submitted to the expertise of their excellencies Pensirolo and Marocchio, leading professors of that university and among the most famous jurists of the present day.

Prince Lodovico Orsini arrived in Padua to discharge his duties concerning the late duke and his widow and to proceed thence to the island of Corfu to take up the post of governor, to which he had been nominated by the Serene Republic.

The first problem to arise between Signora Vittoria and Prince Lodovico was over the late duke's horses, which the prince said did not belong properly speaking to the household effects, but the duchess managed to prove that they should be considered actual effects, and it was decided she should retain the use of them pending a further decision. As guarantor she named Signor Cavalier Soardi da Bergamo, condottiere of the Venetian nobility, a very rich man and among his country's leading figures.

The next difficulty concerned a certain quantity of silver plate, which the late duke had given back to Prince Lodovico as a pledge for a sum of money he had lent the duke. Everything was legally settled, for His Serenity, the Duke of Ferrara, did all he could to see that every one of Prince Orsini's legacies were carried out to the full.

This second matter was decided on 23 December, which was a Sunday. The following night, forty men entered the house of the aforesaid Signora Accoramboni. They were dressed in clothes of coarse linen cut in a bizarre way so that the intruders could not be recognized except by voice. When they spoke to each other they used nicknames.

First they sought the person of the duchess, and, when they found her, one of them said, 'Now you must die.'

Though she begged, he refused even to grant her a single second to commend her soul to God but instantly thrust his dagger beneath her left breast, and, moving the point about in all directions, the assassin several times asked the poor girl to tell him if he had touched her heart. At last she gave up the ghost. All this time, the others were searching for the duchess's brothers, one of whom, Marcello, was saved because they could not find him in the house. The other was stabbed a hundred times. The murderers left the corpses where they fell and the whole household weeping and wailing, and, snatching up the casket which contained the jewels and silver, they departed.

This news quickly reached the Signori Rettori, the magistrates, in Padua, who had the bodies identified and then notified the Venetian authorities.

All Monday, in the palace and at the Church of the Eremitani, people thronged to view the corpses. The curious were moved to compassion, particularly on seeing the duchess's beauty. They wept for her misfortune *et dentibus fremebant* – and gnashed their teeth – against the murderers. But no one yet knew their names.

The Curia was beginning to suspect that the act had been committed on the orders, or at least with the consent of, the aforesaid Prince Lodovico. They summoned him, and as he tried to enter the courtroom of the Most Illustrious Captain with a troop of forty armed men, they barred the door to him and told him he could come in with only three or four. But when these few entered, the others threw themselves in their wake, scattering the guards aside, and they all burst in.

Once before the Most Illustrious Captain, Prince Lodovico complained of the insult to him, alleging that they were treating him as no other sovereign prince had ever been treated. The Most Illustrious Captain asked him if he knew anything about Signora Vittoria's death and what had happened the night before. Prince Lodovico replied yes, and that he had ordered that the matter be brought to law. The tribunal wanted to take down his testimony in writing. He answered that men of his rank were not subject to such a formality nor, equally, should they be interrogated.

Prince Lodovico asked permission to send a courier to Florence with a letter for Prince Virginio Orsini to inform him of the trial and of the crime which had been committed. He showed a letter, which was not the real one, and obtained what he asked for.

But the courier was stopped outside the town and carefully searched. They found the letter Prince Lodovico had shown and a second letter hidden in the man's boot. It ran like this:

To Signor Virginio Orsini
Most Illustrious Signore,
We have carried out what was agreed between us, and in such a way that we have fooled the Most Illustrious Tondini [apparently the name of the magistrate who had interrogated the prince] so thoroughly that I am here considered the finest man in the world. I did the deed myself, so do not fail to send immediately you know who.

This letter caused a sensation among the magistrates, who hastened to send it to Venice. At their command the town gates of Padua were closed and the walls arrayed with soldiers day and night. A notice was posted threatening with dire consequences anyone with knowledge of the assassins who did not tell what he knew to the police. Any of the murderers who could bring evidence against one of the others need not fear, for a sum of money would be paid to him. But at seven o'clock on Christmas Eve Aloise

Bragadino arrived from Venice, with supreme powers from the senate and an order to have arrested dead or alive, at whatever cost, the above-mentioned Prince Lodovico and all his household.

The said Signor Advocate Bragadino, the Signor Capitano, and the Signor Podestà gathered in the fortress. The order was given, under threat of the gallows, to all foot soldiers and cavalry to arm themselves and surround the said Prince Lodovico's palazzo, which was beside the fortress and next to the church of San Agostino on the Arena.

When day broke – it was Christmas Day – an edict was published, exhorting the sons of San Marco to arm themselves and hasten to Prince Lodovico's palazzo. Those without weapons were summoned to the fortress, where they were given all the arms they needed. The edict promised a reward of two thousand ducats to whoever could bring before the tribunal, dead or alive, the said prince, and five hundred ducats for each of his followers. Furthermore, all unarmed men were forbidden to approach the prince's palazzo so as not to obstruct those who were fighting in case the prince decided to launch a sortie.

At the same time cannons and heavy artillery were set up on the old ramparts opposite the palazzo. An equal number were placed on the new ramparts, from which the back of the palazzo could be seen. On this side, the cavalry had been drawn up so that they could manoeuvre freely if necessary. On the river bank benches, wardrobes, carts, and other furniture had been piled to serve as a barricade. It was hoped by these means to hem in the besieged if they tried to march in closed ranks on the people. The barricades would also be used to protect the artillery and soldiers against the arquebuses of the besieged.

Lastly, boats were moored on the river opposite and to the sides of the prince's palazzo. These were crammed with men bearing muskets and other weapons that could harass the enemy if he attempted to break out. At the same time, all roads were barricaded.

While these preparations were under way, a letter expressed in very convincing terms arrrived. In it, the prince complained of being judged guilty and of finding himself treated like an enemy, and even a rebel, before the matter had been brought to trial. This letter was composed by one Liverotto.

On the 27th, three of the town's dignitaries were sent by the magistrates to Prince Lodovico, who had forty men with him in his palazzo, all veteran soldiers experienced in the use of arms. The officials found these men busy loading their arquebuses and erecting barricades made of planks and wet mattresses.

These three gentlemen told the prince that the magistrates were resolved to lay hands on him. They begged him to give himself up, adding that by so doing before anything else happened he could expect some mercy from them. To which Don Lodovico replied that if first the soldiers drawn up round the palazzo were removed he would give himself up to the magistrates together with two or three of his men and deal with the matter under the express condition that they would be free to go home.

The deputation took these proposals written in the prince's own hand and returned to the magistrates, who on the advice of the Most Illustrious Pio Erea in particular and of other nobles present, rejected the conditions.

The deputation went back to the prince and told him that if he did not give himself up, his palazzo would be demolished by cannon fire, to which he replied that he preferred death to submission.

The magistrates gave the battle signal; although they could have destroyed almost the whole house with one blast, they preferred at first to act with some caution to see if those under siege would agree to surrender.

This proved successful, and San Marco was spared a great deal of money which otherwise would have had to be spent on rebuilding the palazzo. All the same, agreement was not unanimous. If Lodovico's men had taken immediate action, without hesitation, and rushed out of the house the outcome would have been very uncertain. They were experienced soldiers. They did not lack weapons or ammunition or courage and, above all, it was greatly to their advantage to win. Looked at from the worst angle, it's bound to be better to die by gunshot than by the executioner's hand. Moreover, who were they fighting against? A feeble troop of besiegers with little experience in weapons, so that, had the prince's men acted thus, the signori would have repented of their clemency and natural goodness.

The besiegers began by bombarding the pillars on the palazzo's façade. Then, aiming higher and higher, they destroyed the wall behind the pillars. Meanwhile, those inside let off volley after volley of musket fire, but the only effect this had was to wound a local man in the shoulder.

'To arms! To arms!' Prince Lodovico cried out in a wild shout. 'To battle! To battle!' He was busy melting down pewter dishes and window leads to make bullets. He seemed poised for a breakout, but the besiegers turned to new measures and brought up their heaviest artillery.

With the first shot they demolished a huge chunk of the house, and a certain Pandolfo Leupratti da Camerino fell into the ruins. He was a brave man and a well-known outlaw. He had been banished from the Papal States, and a reward of four hundred scudi had been put on his head by the distinguished Signor Vitelli, for the death of Vicenzo Vitelli, who had been attacked in his carriage and killed by arquebus and dagger thrust dealt him by Prince Lodovico Orsini through the hands of the aforesaid Pandolfo and his accomplices. Winded by his fall, Pandolfo was unable to move. A servant of the Cai di Lista nobles advanced armed with a pistol. Boldly he cut off Pandolfo's head, which he quickly carried back to the fortress and turned over to the magistrates.

Shortly after, another section of the house was brought down by cannon fire, and at the same time Count Montemellino of Perugia fell with it. He died in the ruins, blown to pieces by the cannon ball.

At this point a certain Colonel Lorenzo, of the Camerino nobility, was seen emerging from the house. A very rich man who had given proof of his courage on several occasions, he was held in high regard by the prince. The colonel resolved not to die unrevenged. He tried to fire his gun, but although the chamber revolved, perhaps by God's intervention the arquebus did not fire, and at that moment his body was pierced by a bullet. The shot had been fired by a poor devil, an assistant teacher at San Michele school. And while to get the promised reward this man was running up to cut off the head, he was preempted by others quicker and stronger, who took the colonel's purse, sword belt, gun, money, rings, and the head.

When those in whom Prince Lodovico placed the greatest trust were dead, he was extremely distressed and seemed incapable of further action.

Signor Filenfi, the prince's chamberlain and secretary, wearing civilian clothes, signalled from the balcony with a white handkerchief that he was giving himself up. He came out and was taken to the fortress, frogmarched in the parlance of war, by Anselmo Suardo, lieutenant of the magistrates.

Questioned on the spot, Filenfi said none of what had happened was in any way his responsibility, because he had arrived in Venice on Christmas Eve and had been there for several days conducting business for the prince.

He was asked how many men the prince had. He replied, 'Twenty or thirty.' He was asked for their names and replied that there were eight or ten who, being men of rank, ate like him at the prince's table, and he knew their names. But the others, adventurers and vagabonds, had only been with the prince a short time and were not known to him.

He named thirty men, including Liverotto's brother. A little later the artillery, which was on the ramparts, began to fire. Soldiers took up positions in buildings adjoining the prince's palazzo to prevent his men from escaping. The prince, who had run the same risks as the two whose deaths we have described, told those who were with him to hold out until they saw a message in his own hand together with a certain signal. After this, he gave himself up to the Anselmo Suardo we have already mentioned. And since he could not make his way by carriage, as was prescribed, owing to the throngs of people at the street barricades, it was decided that he should proceed on foot.

Surrounded by Marcello Accoramboni's men, he walked with condottieri at his sides as well as with

Lieutenant Suardo and other captains and towns-men, all of them well armed. Then came an armed troop of men and soldiers from the town. Prince Lodovico was dressed in brown, his stiletto at his side and his cloak flung over his arm in a debonair manner. With a disdainful smile, he remarked, 'If I had entered the fray', meaning that if he had he would have carried the day. Brought before the mag-istrates, he greeted them and said, indicating Signor Anselmo, 'Sirs, I am this gentleman's prisoner and I am very angry at what has happened, none of which was my fault.'

When the captain ordered the stiletto which hung at the prince's hip to be removed, Lodovico propped himself against a balustrade and began to clip his nails with a small pair of scissors he found there.

He was asked how many people he had in his house. He named, among others, Colonel Liverotto and Count Montemellino, whom we have men-tioned previously, adding that he would give ten thousand scudi to buy back the life of the one, and for the other he would give his own blood. He asked to be put in a place appropriate to a man of his standing. When this was granted, he wrote to his men in his own hand, recommending them to surrender, and he gave his ring as a sign. He told Signor Anselmo that he was handing over to him his sword and gun, begging that when the weapons in his palazzo were found the signore would use them for love of the prince, since they were gentlemen's weapons and not those of a common soldier.

The soldiers entered the palazzo, searched it from top to bottom, and on the spot rounded up the prince's men, who were thirty-four in number. They were then led in pairs to the palazzo's prison. The dead were left to be scavenged by dogs, and everyone hastened to give an account of the affair to Venice.

It was noticed that many of Prince Lodovico's soldiers, accomplices after the fact, were missing. Edicts were issued forbidding anyone to harbour them under threat of having their houses demolished and all their goods confiscated. Anyone who denounced them would receive fifty scudi. In this way, several were captured.

A frigate has been sent from Venice to Crete, carrying an order to Signor Latino Orsini to come at once on a matter of the gravest urgency and it is thought that he will lose his position.

Yesterday morning, Santo Stefano's Day, everyone expected to see Prince Lodovico put to death or to hear that he had been strangled in prison. There was widespread surprise that this did not take place, considering that he was not a bird to remain long in a cage. But on the following night the trial took place, and on San Giovanni's Day, just before dawn, it was heard that the prince had been strangled and that he had died well prepared. His body was quickly taken to the cathedral, accompanied by the clergy of that church and by Jesuit priests, where it was displayed all day on a table in the centre of the church to serve as a spectacle for the populace and a mirror for the unwise.

The next day the body was taken to Venice, as the prince had stipulated in his will, and there he was buried.

On Saturday two of his men were hanged. The first and more important was Furio Savorgnano; the other, a person of low birth. On Monday, which was the last day but one of the year, thirteen men were hanged, many of them nobles. Two others, one called Captain Splendiano and the other Count Paganello, were led through the square and slowly torn with red-hot pincers. When they reached the place of execution they were bludgeoned, their heads smashed, and they were quartered while still almost alive. These men were nobles and before they had taken to crime they had been very rich. Count Paganello was said to be the assassin who had killed Signora Vittoria Accoramboni in the cruel way I have described.

To counter this, in his aforesaid letter Prince Lodovico swore that he himself had done the deed. Perhaps he had claimed this out of the same pride he showed in Rome when he had Vitelli assassinated or as a way of currying Prince Virginio Orsini's favour.

After he had received the death blow, Count Paganello was stabbed several times under the left breast in an attempt to touch his heart, as he had done to the poor lady. Owing to this, rivers of blood flowed from his breast. To the astonishment of all, he lived a further half hour. He was a man of forty-five who exhibited great strength.

Gallows have been erected to dispatch the remaining nineteen on the first day after the holiday. But as the executioner is very tired and the people in a frenzy from having witnessed so many deaths, the execution is postponed for two days. It is thought that none of the accused will be left alive. It is possible that the only exception amongst Prince Lodovico's men may be Signor Filenfi, his chamberlain, who is doing his utmost to establish that he had no part in the affair.

Not even the oldest citizens of Padua can remember an occasion when so many people were more justly put to death at the same time. The Venetian signori have acquired fame and a good reputation amongst the most civilized nations.

Added by another hand

Francesco Filenfi, secretary and chamberlain, was sentenced to fifteen years in prison. The cup-bearer (*copiere*) Onorio Adami da Fermo, along with two others, to one year in prison. Seven others were condemned to the galleys, with leg irons, and finally seven were released.

THE CENCI

(1599)

I

Molière's Don Juan is certainly a philanderer, but first and foremost he's a man of breeding. While he gives in to the irresistible urge that draws him to pretty women, above all he is set on conforming to a certain ideal. He wants to be the man most admired at the court of a witty, debonair young king.

Mozart's Don Giovanni is closer to nature and not so French. He is less concerned with what others think. In the words of d'Aubigné's Baron de Fœniste, he is not for ever worrying about 'appearances'. We have only two portraits of the Italian Don Juan as he must have looked in that beautiful country in the sixteenth century at the beginning of the Renaissance.

One of these two portraits I cannot discuss, for our century is too strait-laced. It's worth bearing in mind Lord Byron's great phrase, which I have often heard quoted – 'this age of cant'. Hypocrisy, which is so tiresome it takes in no one, has one huge merit in that it gives fools something to talk about. They are scandalized if one dares mention such-and-such, if one dares laugh at something else, etc. The drawback is that this greatly limits the field of history. If the reader has the good taste to allow me, I will give him in all humility an historical account of the second of these Don Juans, of whom, in 1837, one may speak. His name was Francesco Cenci.

For a Don Juan to exist, there must be hypocrisy. The Don Juan character is an effect whose cause has no root in the ancient world. Religion in those days was a celebration, urging men to pleasure. Why would it stigmatize anyone who made a particular pleasure his sole concern? The government advocated abstinence, but only forbade activities which could harm the country – that is to say, the obvious interests of all and not those which would harm the individual who indulged in them.

Therefore in Athens any man with a taste for women and with a lot of money could be a Don Juan. No one would have objected. No one would have claimed that this life was a vale of tears and that there was any good in suffering.

I do not think that an Athenian Don Juan could have descended into crime as rapidly as a Don Juan in the monarchies of today. A great part of the latter's pleasure consists in flouting convention, a taste that began in his youth when he thought he was merely defying hypocrisy.

To break the law in a monarchy like that of Louis XV, to open fire on a roofer and bring him toppling down from his rooftop – is that not proof that one rubs shoulders with the prince, that one is better bred, and that one doesn't give a damn for middle-class law? Is not to fly in the face of the law the first step, the first test, of every little would-be Don Juan?

Nowadays in France women are no longer in fashion, which is why French Don Juans are rare. Where they do exist they always start out by seeking the most natural of pleasures, while making a virtue of defying the religious convictions of their contemporaries, which seem to them meaningless. It is not until later, when he begins to become perverted, that our Don Juan finds exquisite pleasure in defying opinions that seem even to him both right and reasonable.

Such a progression must have been very difficult in classical Greece, and it is only under the Roman emperors after Tiberius and Capri that we find libertines who love depravity for its own sake – that is, for the pleasure of defying the reasonable beliefs of their contemporaries.

I therefore attribute the emergence of a satanically inspired Don Juan to the Christian religion. It was this religion that taught the world that the soul of a poor slave or a gladiator was equal to that of Caesar himself. So we must thank Christianity for the rise of delicate feelings. I am sure, however, that sooner or later such feelings would have made themselves felt in the hearts of the people. The Aeneid is considerably more tender than the Iliad.

Jesus' doctrine was the same as that of his contemporaries, the Arab philosophers. The only new element introduced into the world as a result of St Paul's preachings was a priesthood set completely apart from the rest of the people and even with opposing interests.

This body of priests concentrated its efforts on cultivating and strengthening religious fervour. They invented rituals and practices to stir the hearts of people of all classes, from the simple shepherd to the world-weary courtier. They were able to create a link between their preachings and the sweet impressions of early childhood. They did not allow the least epidemic or the greatest misfortune to pass by without using the calamity to increase fear and religious fervour or at least to build a fine church, such as the Salute, in Venice.

The existence of such a body of priests led to the much admired occasion when, without physical force, Pope St Leo resisted the terrible Attila and his barbarian hordes, who had just wreaked havoc in China, Persia, and Gaul.

Thus, as with that absolute power tempered by song known as the French monarchy, religion has brought about a great many wondrous things that the world would never have seen had it not produced these two institutions.

Among the many things both good and bad but always unusual and extraordinary that would have astonished Aristotle, Polybius, Augustus, and other distinguished men of the ancient world, I unhesitatingly place the wholly modern character of Don Juan. I consider this character a product of the ascetic institutions created by the popes who came after Luther, since Leo X and his court (1506) to some extent followed the precepts of Athenian religion.

Molière's *Don Juan* was first performed on 15 February 1665, at the beginning of Louis XIV's reign. This prince was not in the least devout; nevertheless, the ecclesiastical censors struck out the scene with the poor man in the forest. To attain power, the censors managed to persuade the exceptionally ignorant young king that the word Jansenist was synonymous with Republican.

The original Don Juan is by Tirso de Molina, a Spaniard. An Italian troupe produced an adaptation of it in Paris in about 1664, thereby provoking a stormy reaction. It is probably the most frequently staged comedy in the world. In it we find the devil, love, fear of hell, an exalted passion for a woman – all, that is, which is most sweet and most terrible in the eyes of every man above the savage state.

It is not surprising that the character of Don Juan was introduced into literature by a Spanish poet. Love plays a dominant role in the life of that people. In Spain love is a serious passion, one which demands sacrifices from all other passions including, believe it or not, vanity! It's the same in Germany and Italy. Only France, in fact, is completely free of this passion, which makes foreigners get up to such folly – for instance, marrying a poor girl on the excuse that she is pretty or that you are in love with her. In France girls who are not pretty have no lack of suitors. We are a prudent people. Elsewhere plain girls are compelled to become nuns, and that is why convents are so indispensable in Spain. Girls do not have dowries in that country, and this law has maintained the ascendency of love. In France, however, love has fled to the attics – that is, to the girls who do not marry with the intervention of a family solicitor.

We can leave out Lord Byron's Don Juan, for he is only a Faublas, a handsome, aimless young man upon whom all kinds of improbable delights are showered.

Therefore, it is in Italy, and in the sixteenth century, that this remarkable character must have made his first appearance. It is in Italy, and in the seventeenth century, that a princess partaking of an ice cream with extreme pleasure one evening after a very hot day said, 'What a pity this is not a sin.'

In my opinion this notion forms the basis of the Don Juan character, and, obviously, the Christian religion is necessary to it. At which point a Neapolitan writer cries, 'Is it nothing to defy the heavens and to believe at the same time that the heavens can reduce you to ash? Herein lies the extreme sensual pleasure of having a devout mistress, filled with piety, who is well aware that she is doing wrong and asks God's pardon as passionately as she sins.'

Let us consider a highly wilful Christian, a man born in Rome at the time when the stern Pius V had just reinstated or invented a mass of petty practices utterly alien to that natural morality that believes virtue only lies in that which is useful to mankind. An inexorable inquisition, so inexorable that it didn't last long in Italy and had to take itself off to Spain, has just been re-established and is instilling fear in everyone. For several years dire penalties were exacted for the non-observance or public contempt for such infinitesimal practices now elevated to the rank of sacred duty. Our character would have shrugged his shoulders on seeing everyone tremble in the face of the Inquisition's strict rules. 'Well,' he would have thought, 'I am the richest man in Rome, the capital of the world, and I shall also be the boldest. I shall make fools of all these respectable citizens who so little resemble anyone worthy of respect.' To be a Don Juan, a man must have courage and a quick, uncluttered mind that sees clearly into the motives behind a person's actions.

Francesco Cenci would have thought, 'How can I, a Roman, born in Rome in 1527 during those same six months when the Lutheran soldiers of the Bourbon high constable's court were committing the most appalling profanities upon the holiest places, bring my bravery to public attention and give myself, as profoundly as possible, the pleasure of flying in the face of public opinion? How can I shock my doltish contemporaries? How can I give myself that keen thrill of feeling different from the crowd?'

It would not enter the head of a Roman, and a medieval Roman at that, to restrict himself to these words. There is no country where bold words are held in more contempt than in Italy.

Francesco Cenci was a man who might have thought this way. On 15 September 1598 he was murdered as his daughter and wife looked on. Nothing pleasant has come down to us about this Don Juan. His character has been in no way softened or toned down by any desire on his part to be a well-bred man, like Molière's Don Juan. He never gave a thought to others except to impress them with his superiority, to make use of them to further his own ends, or to hate them. Our Don Juan takes no pleasure in compassion, in gentle dreams, or the illusions of a tender heart. His pleasures have to be conquests that can be seen by others and cannot be ignored. He needs the list which the insolent Leporello waves in front of poor Elvira's eyes.

Our Roman Don Juan would never have done anything so clumsy as to give away the key to his character or to confide in a lackey, like Molière's Don Juan. He never had a confidant and only spoke such words as were necessary to achieve his ends. No one ever saw him in those moments of real tenderness and delightful merriment that make us forgive Mozart's Don Juan. In a word, the portrait I am going to draw is appalling.

Personally I would not have chosen to portray this character. I would have been satisfied with merely studying him because he is satanic rather than intriguing. But I assure you I was begged to do so by my travelling companions, to whom I could refuse nothing. In 1823, I was lucky enough to see Italy in the company of some delightful people whom I shall never forget. I was deeply affected, as were they, by the exquisite portrait of Beatrice Cenci that we saw in Rome at the Palazzo Barberini.

The picture gallery of this palazzo has now been reduced to but seven or eight paintings, four of which are masterpieces. First, there is the portrait of the famous Fornarina, Raphael's mistress, by Raphael himself. This portrait, over whose authenticity there can be no doubt, for contemporary copies can be found, is quite different from the face in the Florentine gallery, which is said to be Raphael's portrait and has been engraved under his name by Morghen. The Florentine portrait itself is not even by Raphael. In courtesy to a great name, the reader will perhaps forgive this short digression.

The second precious portrait in the Barberini gallery is by Guido Reni. It is the portrait of Beatrice Cenci, many bad prints of which are in existence. The great painter has draped a light piece of material round Beatrice's neck and shoulders and bound her head in a turban. He was afraid of pushing realism to the point of gruesomeness by painting an exact picture of the costume she'd had made for her execution, with the dishevelled hair of a poor sixteen-year-old girl who has just given in to utter despair. The face is calm and lovely, the expression gentle, and the eyes very large. They have the startled look of a person who has been surprised as she wept hot tears. Her hair is fair and very beautiful. This face has none of the Roman arrogance and awareness of its own power that one often catches in the confident expression of a daughter of the Tiber, *di una figlia del Tevere*, as they proudly call themselves. Unfortunately the half-tones have turned to a brick-red over the two hundred and thirty-eight long years that separate us from the catastrophe which I am about to relate.

The third portrait in the Barberini gallery is that of Lucrezia Petroni, Beatrice's stepmother, who was executed with her. In her natural beauty and pride she looks the true Roman matron. Her features are imposing, and the flesh tints are of an astonishing whiteness; the eyebrows are black and strongly marked; the expression is haughty and at the same time full of voluptuousness. This contrasts beautifully with the gentle, candid, almost Germanic face of her stepdaughter.

The fourth portrait glows with rich lifelike colours.

It is one of Titian's masterpieces, a Greek slave, the mistress of the famous Doge Barbarigo.

Almost all foreigners on arriving in Rome have themselves taken at once to the Barberini gallery. They are drawn, particularly the women, by the portraits of Beatrice Cenci and her stepmother. I shared the common curiosity. Then, like everyone else, I tried to gain access to certain parts of their famous trial. Anyone who has the influence to do so will be amazed, I think, on reading these accounts – which are all in Latin except for the replies of the accused – to find almost no explanation of the facts. The reason is that no one in Rome in 1599 was unacquainted with the facts. I bought permission to copy a contemporary account. I thought I could make a translation which would in no way offend propriety. At least this translation can be read aloud to French ladies in 1823. It is well understood that a translator ceases to be faithful when he no longer can be, since horror would quickly prevail over simple curiosity.

The sad role of the genuine Don Juan – he who seeks to conform to no model and who only considers the opinion of others in order to shock – is revealed here in all its horror. His outrageous crimes force two unhappy women to have him killed before their very eyes. These two are his wife and daughter, and the reader will not dare to decide whether they were guilty. Their contemporaries felt they should not have died.

I am convinced that the tragedy of Galeotto Manfredi (who was killed by his wife, a subject treated by the great poet Monti), and many other domestic tragedies of the sixteenth century, which are less well known and scarcely mentioned in local histories of various Italian towns, ended with a scene similar to that in La Petrella castle. Here is my translation of a contemporary account. It is in Roman Italian and was set down on 14 September 1599.

A TRUE ACCOUNT

of the deaths of Giacomo Cenci, Beatrice Cenci, and Lucrezia Petroni Cenci, their stepmother, executed for the crime of patricide last Saturday, 11 September 1599, during the reign of the Holy Father Pope Clement VIII, Aldobrandini.

The monstrous life which Roman-born Francesco Cenci, one of our richest fellow citizens, has always led has finally brought about his destruction. He has carried off to an early death his sons, strong, brave young men, and his daughter Beatrice. Although barely sixteen when sent to her death four days ago, she was nevertheless considered one of the most beautiful women in the Papal States and in all Italy. News is spreading that Signor Guido Reni, a pupil of the famous Bologna school, wished to paint a portrait of poor Beatrice last Friday – the very eve, that is, of the execution. If this great artist has carried out the task as successfully as the other paintings he has produced in the capital, posterity will have some idea of this remarkable girl's beauty. So that posterity should also retain some memory of her unparalled misfortunes, and of the astonishing fortitude with which this truly Roman soul withstood them, I have decided to record what I have learned of the events which led up to her death and what I saw on the day of her glorious tragedy.

The people who gave me my information occupied positions that allowed them access to the most secret details of the case, which to this day are not generally known in Rome, although for the past six weeks people have talked of nothing but the Cenci trial. I am going to write with considerable freedom, as I am assured that I will be able to lodge my account in respectable archives, from which it will only be removed after my lifetime. My only regret is to have to impugn (but the truth will out) the innocence of poor Beatrice Cenci, who was as loved and respected by all who knew her as her vile father was loathed and execrated.

This man, who was undeniably endowed by heaven with extraordinary shrewdness and caprice, was the son of Monsignor Cenci, who was promoted to the position of treasurer – that is, minister of finance – under Pius V, Ghislieri. That saintly pope who was, as we know, preoccupied with a justified hatred of heresy and the re-establishment of his excellent Inquisition, had nothing but contempt for the temporal administration of his State. It was thus that Monsignor Cenci, who was treasurer for several years before 1572, found the means to leave to the appalling man who was his son and the father of Beatrice, a net income of a hundred and sixty thousand scudi.

In addition to this huge fortune, Francesco Cenci had a reputation for courage and shrewdness which, in his youth, no other Roman could match. This reputation stood him in such good stead at the Papal Court and amongst the people as a whole, that the crimes which were beginning to be attributed to him were only of the type which the world readily forgives. Many Romans also remembered with bitter regret the freedom of thought and action which they had enjoyed in the time of Leo X, who was taken from us in 1513, and under Paul III, who died in 1549. During the reign of this latter pope, young Francesco Cenci's name began to be linked with certain unusual love affairs pursued in ways that were even more unusual.

In the reign of Paul III, a period when there was still some freedom of speech, many people said that Francesco Cenci was particularly obsessed with strange activities which might give him *peripezie di nuova idea*, new and disturbing sensations. These suppositions were based on entries found in his account books, such as this one: 'For the exploits and *peripezie* at Toscanello, three thousand five hundred scudi, *e non fu caro* – and it was not expensive.'

In other Italian towns it is perhaps not realized that in Rome our fate and our way of life change according to the character of the reigning pope. Thus for thirteen years, under good Pope Gregory XIII, Buoncompagni, anything was permitted in Rome. If a man wanted to have an enemy stabbed, he would not be prosecuted so long as he went about it in a discreet manner. This excess of leniency was followed by an excess of severity over the five-year reign of the great Sixtus V. It has been said of him, as was said of the Emperor Augustus, that either he should never have come to the throne or else he should have stayed there for ever. At that time we witnessed executions of unfortunate wretches for assassinations or poisonings forgotten for ten years, which the perpetrators had had the ill luck to confess to Cardinal Montalto, now Sixtus V.

It was chiefly in the reign of Gregory XIII that Francesco Cenci's affairs became the subject of widespread discussion. He had married a very rich woman, as suited a man of his standing, who died after giving him seven children. Shortly after her death he took as a second wife one Lucrezia Petroni, a woman of unusual beauty, admired for the dazzling whiteness of her complexion but a little too plump, a defect common amongst Roman women. He had no children by Lucrezia.

The least of the vices imputed to Francesco Cenci was a predilection for perverted love affairs; the greatest was that of not believing in God. Throughout his entire life he was never seen to enter a church.

Thrown into prison thrice for these perverted affairs, he managed to get himself released by giving two hundred thousand scudi to individuals enjoying the patronage of the twelve popes who succeeded each other during Cenci's lifetime.

Francesco Cenci already had greying hair when I met him. This was during the reign of Pope Buoncompagni, when a man could get away with anything he dared to do. Cenci was about five feet four inches tall, well built, although somewhat thin. He was considered extremely strong, a rumour he may have spread himself. He had large expressive eyes, though the upper lids drooped a little too much. His nose was too large and prominent. His lips were thin and his smile gracious. This smile could become terrible when he glared at his enemies. If he were in the least upset or irritated he would tremble so wildly that he could scarcely control himself. As a young man I saw him riding from Rome to Naples, doubtless for one of his little amorous adventures. He was going through the San Germano and Faggiola woods, quite unconcerned about brigands, and he made the journey, it was said, in fewer than twenty hours. He always travelled alone without letting anyone know beforehand. When his first horse tired, he bought or stole another. If anyone put the slightest obstacle in his path, nothing would prevent Cenci from stabbing that person with his dagger. Indeed, it is true to say that when I was a young man – that is, when he was forty-eight or fifty – no one was bold enough to stand up to him. His main delight lay in defying his enemies.

He was well known along the highways and by-ways of the Papal States. He paid generously but he was also quite capable of sending hired assassins to murder anyone who offended him, even two or three months after the offence had been committed.

During the whole of his long life, his only virtuous deed was to build a church dedicated to San Tommaso in the courtyard of his huge palazzo near the Tiber. Yet he was driven to this by the extraordinary desire to have beneath his eyes the tombs of all his children, for whom he had an immense and unnatural hatred, even during their tenderest years, when they could not have offended him in any way.

'That's where I want to put them all,' he often said with a bitter laugh to the workmen he employed to build his church. He sent the three eldest, Giacomo, Cristoforo, and Rocco, to study at the University of Salamanca, in Spain. Once they arrived in that far-off land, he took an evil delight in dispatching them no allowances, so that the unfortunate young men, after writing numerous letters to him, all of which remained unanswered, were reduced to the bleak necessity of borrowing small sums of money or of begging at the roadside.

Back in Rome they found a father who was harsher, more severe and angrier than ever, and who despite his vast wealth would neither clothe them nor give them money enough to buy the cheapest food. The unfortunate youths were obliged to appeal to the pope, who forced Francesco Cenci to grant them a small allowance. With this pittance, they cut themselves off from him.

Soon afterwards, as a result of his perverted love affairs, Francesco was imprisoned for the third and last time, at which juncture his three sons begged an audience with the Holy Father, the pope now in office, and together besought him to have their father put to death for, as they said, having dishonoured their family. Clement VIII greatly wished to do so, but he refused to obey his first instinct, not wanting to satisfy such unnatural children, and he sent them in shame from his presence.

As we noted earlier, their father got himself out of prison by giving a large sum of money to anyone who would aid him. We must assume that the extreme step taken by his three eldest sons only served to increase further the hatred that he bore towards his children. He cursed them at every turn, both the elder and the little ones, and every day he rained blows with his stick upon his two poor daughters, who lived with him in his palazzo.

The elder girl, although closely watched, went to the enormous lengths of arranging for a plea to be presented to the pope, in which she entreated His Holiness to marry her off or to place her in a convent.

Clement VIII took pity on her distress and married
her to Carlo Gabrielli of the noble family of Gubbio.
His Holiness forced her father to give her a handsome dowry.

At this unexpected blow, Francesco Cenci went
into a raging passion, and to prevent his younger
daughter Beatrice from any idea of following her sister's example when she grew older, he confined her
to one of the apartments in his huge palazzo. There
no one was allowed to see Beatrice, then scarcely
fourteen years old and already in the full flower of a
ravishing beauty. She had, moreover, a gaiety, a simplicity, and a lively wit that I have seen in no one
else. Francesco Cenci himself brought food to her. It
is thought that it was then that this monster fell in
love with her, or pretended to fall in love with her,
so as to torment his wretched daughter. He often
spoke to her of the treachery of her elder sister, and,
working himself into a fury by his own words, ended
by raining blows upon Beatrice.

Meanwhile, Rocco Cenci, his son, was killed by
a pork butcher, and the following year Cristoforo
Cenci was killed by Paolo Corso, of Massa. On this
occasion their father revealed his godlessness, for he
refused to pay as much as a single *baiocco* for the
candles. On hearing of the fate of his son Cristoforo,
he cried out that he would never have a moment's
happiness until all his children were buried and as
soon as the last one died he would set his palazzo on

fire as a sign of his joy. Rome was astounded by all this but could believe anything of a man who made a virtue of defying the whole world and the pope himself.

Nor did any of this satisfy him. With threats and by force he tried to violate his own daughter Beatrice, who was now grown up and a beauty. Shamelessly, he placed himself in her bed, completely naked. He strolled with her through the halls of his palazzo, he himself still quite naked. Then he led her to his wife's bed, so that by the lamplight poor Lucrezia could see what he did to Beatrice.

He gave the poor girl to believe such a fearful heresy that I scarcely dare relate it. He said that when a father lay with his own daughter, the children which were born would automatically become saints and that all the greatest saints most revered by the church were born in this way – that is to say, that their maternal grandfather was their father.

When Beatrice resisted his infamous lust he beat her cruelly, until the poor girl, unable to sustain so miserable a life, decided to follow her sister's example. She wrote a detailed petition to the Holy Father, but it is believed that Francesco Cenci must have taken precautions because this petition apparently never reached the hands of His Holiness. At any rate, it was impossible to find the document in the office of the Memoriali, when Beatrice was in prison and her lawyer urgently needed it. The document might have provided evidence of the outrageous excesses which were committed in the castle of La Petrella. Was it not clear to everyone that Beatrice Cenci had a legitimate defence? That daybook also mentioned the name of Lucrezia, Beatrice's stepmother.

Francesco Cenci learned of his daughter's plan, and we can imagine the fury with which he redoubled his ill-treatment of these two wretched women.

Their lives became absolutely unbearable, and it was then that, realizing they could hope for nothing from the justice of the sovereign, whose courtiers had been won over by Francesco's rich gifts, they conceived the idea which brought about their downfall. It did, however, have the one advantage of putting an end to their suffering in this world.

We should understand that the renowned Monsignor Guerra often frequented the Palazzo Cenci. A tall, exceptionally good-looking man, he was endowed with a singular ability to do with a special grace anything he set his mind to. It was thought that he was in love with Beatrice and intended to give up the cloth and marry her, but, although he took great pains to hide his feelings, he was detested by Francesco Cenci, who accused him of having been in league with all his children. When Monsignor Guerra learned that Signor Cenci was away, he went up to the ladies' apartments and spent several hours chatting with them, listening to their grievances and to their tale of the unbelievable treatment to which both had been subjected. Apparently it was Beatrice who first dared voice aloud to Monsignor Guerra the plan upon which they had decided.

In the course of time he made a pact with them and, strongly urged several times by Beatrice, he finally agreed to communicate their proposal to Giacomo Cenci, without whose consent nothing could be done, as he was the eldest brother and head of the house after Francesco.

It was not difficult for them to draw Giacomo into their conspiracy. He had been very badly treated by his father, who gave him no help, an extremely sore point with Giacomo, who was married and had six children. Monsignor Guerra's apartments were chosen as the place where they would meet to discuss the best way to kill Francesco Cenci. The affair was arranged in the most seemly fashion, and the stepmother's and the young girl's votes were taken at every step. When they finally decided what to do, they chose two of Francesco's vassals, who nursed a deadly hatred towards him. One of them was called Marzio. He was a good-hearted man, strongly attached to Francesco's unhappy children, and, to please them, he agreed to take part in the patricide. Olimpio, the second man, had been appointed warden of the fortress of La Petrella, in the Kingdom of Naples, by Prince Colonna, but Francesco Cenci had used his powerful influence with the prince to oust Olimpio.

Everything was arranged with the two men. Francesco Cenci had announced that to escape the unhealthy climate of Rome, he would spend the following summer at La Petrella, and so the assassins decided to call on a dozen Neapolitan brigands. Olimpio took on the job of recruiting them. It was decided that they would hide in the forest around La Petrella, where they would be informed of the moment Francesco Cenci set off from Rome. They would then seize him as he passed on the road and announce to his family that he would be released upon payment of a substantial ransom. The children would then have to return to Rome to collect the sum demanded by the brigands. They would pretend to be unable to raise the money quickly, and the brigands, seeing no sign of the money and true to their threats, would put Francesco Cenci to death. In this way no one would suspect the true authors of the murder.

But when summer came and Francesco Cenci left Rome for La Petrella, the spy who was to have given warning of his departure was late in informing the bandits in the forest, which gave them no time to get down to the highway. Cenci reached La Petrella unharmed. The brigands, tired of waiting for so uncertain a prey, went off to steal elsewhere on their own account.

Cenci, for his part, crafty old man that he was, never ran the risk of leaving his fortress. His bad temper increasing with the infirmities of old age, which were unbearable to him, he redoubled the atrocious treatment that he forced the two poor women to undergo. He claimed they were taking delight in his weakness.

At the end of her tether from the horrible things which she had to suffer, Beatrice summoned Marzio and Olimpio to come to the foot of the fortress walls. During the night, while her father slept, she spoke to them through a low window and threw them letters addressed to Monsignor Guerra.

By means of these letters it was arranged that Monsignor Guerra would promise Marzio and Olimpio a thousand scudi if they would take on the job of killing Francesco Cenci. A third of the sum would be paid by Monsignor Guerra in Rome before the deed, and the remaining two-thirds by Lucrezia and Beatrice when, after the deed was done, they were mistresses of the Cenci coffers.

It was further agreed that the act would take place on the day of the Madonna's nativity, and with this in view the two men were stealthily let into the fortress. But Lucrezia was restrained by the reverence due to the Feast of the Madonna, and she persuaded Beatrice to change the day so as not to commit a double sin.

Thus it was on 9 September 1598, in the evening, that the mother and daughter managed with considerable skill to administer opium to Francesco Cenci, a man who was so difficult to trick. At which he fell into a deep slumber.

Towards midnight Beatrice let Marzio and Olimpio into the fortress. Then Lucrezia took them to the room where the old man lay sound asleep. There they were left to perform what had been agreed, while the women waited in a nearby room. Suddenly they observed the two men emerge, pale-faced and distraught.

'What's happened?' asked the women.

'It seemed base and despicable to kill a poor old man in his sleep. We took pity on him and couldn't do it.'

At this excuse, Beatrice was filled with indignation and began to berate them, saying, 'Call yourselves men? You haven't the courage to kill a sleeping man. How would you face him if he were awake? You dare do this and then take money for it? Well, since your cowardice forces me, I'll kill my father myself. And as for you two, you won't live long.'

Emboldened by these stormy words and fearing some loss in the agreed payment, Marzio and Olimpio returned to the room, followed by the women. One of the hired killers had a large nail, which he placed vertically over the sleeping man's eye and then the other, who had a hammer, drove the nail into the victim's head. They then drove another nail into his throat, at which the poor soul, burdened with so many recent sins, was whisked off to hell. The body thrashed about, but in vain.

The deed done, the young girl gave Olimpio a large purse full of silver. She gave Marzio a cloak of gold brocade, which had belonged to her father, and then she sent them away.

Left alone, the women first withdrew the large nail from the corpse's head and then the one from the neck. They wrapped the body in a bed sheet and dragged it through a series of rooms to a gallery that looked out onto a small disused garden. From there, they threw the body onto an elderberry tree which grew in that desolate spot. As there were some privies at the far end of this gallery, they hoped that when the old man's body was found the next day, caught in the tree's branches, everyone would think that on his way to the privy his foot had slipped and he had fallen.

Events turned out exactly as had been anticipated. In the morning, when the body was found, an uproar arose in the castle. The women made haste to scream and moan and bewail the death of a father and husband. But filled with the recklessness of insulted modesty, young Beatrice lacked the prudence necessary for survival. Early that morning she had given the woman who washed the castle's linen a blood-drenched sheet, telling her not to be surprised at such large stains because she had been bleeding heavily all night. Thus, for the moment, all was well.

Francesco Cenci was given an honourable burial, and the women returned to Rome to enjoy the peace for which they had yearned so long in vain. They felt happier than they had ever been, for they had no idea of what was happening in Naples.

Divine justice would not let so heinous a patricide go unpunished, and it moved in such a way that, as soon as the events in the castle of La Petrella became known in Rome, the chief justice became suspicious and sent a royal commissioner to look at the body and have the suspected persons arrested.

The commissioner had everyone who lived in the castle detained. They were all taken to Naples in chains. Nothing in their depositions would have aroused suspicion had it not been for the washer-woman, who told how she had received from Beatrice a sheet, or sheets, covered in blood. She was asked whether Beatrice had tried to explain the large stains. She replied that Beatrice had mentioned a natural indisposition. She was asked if such large stains could result from such an indisposition. She replied that they could not, that the blood stains were of too bright a red.

This information was sent on the spot to the authorities in Rome. Nevertheless, several months went by before anyone there dreamed of having Francesco Cenci's children arrested. Lucrezia, Beatrice, and Giacomo could have saved themselves a thousand times, either by going to Florence under the pretext of making a pilgrimage or by embarking from Civita-vecchia. But God kept this inspired idea from them.

On learning of what had happened in Naples, Monsignor Guerra instantly sent out some men with orders to kill Marzio and Olimpio. But they were only able to kill Olimpio, in Terni. The Neapolitan officials had arrested Marzio and taken him to Naples, where at once he admitted everything.

This fateful deposition was immediately dispatched to the Roman courts, which finally decided to have Giacomo and Bernardo Cenci arrested and sent to the prison of Corte Savella, and with them Lucrezia, the widow. Beatrice was kept under guard in her father's palazzo by a large corps of secret police. Marzio was taken to Naples and he too was put into Savella prison. There he was confronted by the two women, who categorically denied everything, and Beatrice in particular refused to recognize the bro-caded cloak she had given to Marzio. Smitten with admiration for the outstanding beauty and astonishing eloquence with which the young girl replied to the prosecutor, Marzio denied everything he had admitted in Naples. Interrogated, he said nothing and chose to die under torture, a fitting homage to Beatrice's beauty.

After his death, as the facts of the killing had in no way been established, the prosecutor could not find sufficient evidence to put either of Cenci's sons or the two women to the torture. All four were taken to the Castel Sant' Angelo, where they spent four very peaceful months.

The case seemed over, and no one in Rome doubted that the beautiful, brave girl who had inspired such lively interest, would soon be freed, when, as ill luck would have it, some officers of the law arrested the brigand who had killed Olimpio at Terni. Brought to Rome, the man confessed everything. Compromised by the brigand's confession, Monsignor Guerra was summoned to appear at once before the court. Imprisonment was certain, death quite probable. But this estimable man, endowed by fortune with remarkable resourcefulness, managed to escape in a manner little short of a miracle. He was considered the most outstanding man at the Papal Court, and he was too well known in Rome to hope to save himself. Moreover, the city gates were well guarded, and his house was watched, probably from the minute the summons had been delivered. The Monsignor was very tall, with a light complexion, a handsome blond beard, and a fine head of hair of the same colour.

In the blink of an eye, he seized a charcoal-seller, took his clothes, shaved off his own hair and beard, dyed his face, bought two donkeys, and set off to wander the streets of Rome, limping and selling charcoal. With great skill he made himself look coarse and dull and he went around crying his wares, his mouth full of bread and onions, while hundreds of secret police searched for him not only in Rome but along all the highways. Eventually, when his new face was well known to most of the secret police, he ventured to leave Rome, still driving his two charcoal-laden donkeys before him. He came across several groups of police, who made no attempt to stop him. Since then, only a single letter has been received from him. His mother sent money to him to Marseilles, and it is assumed that he is fighting as a mercenary in France.

The Terni assassin's confession and Monsignor Guerra's flight, which produced a great sensation in Rome, revived suspicions and strengthened the evidence against the Cenci family so that they were removed from the Castel Sant' Angelo and taken back to Savella prison.

When put to the torture, the two brothers fell far short of matching the nobility of the brigand Marzio. They were so weak as to confess everything. Signora Lucrezia Petroni, used to the softness and ease of a life of luxury, could not bear the idea of interrogation by being strung up. She revealed all she knew.

But it was quite different with Beatrice Cenci, a young girl who was full of spirit and courage. Neither Judge Moscati's kind words or threats swayed her. She bore the torture of the rope with perfect equanimity and bravery. The judge could not elicit a single reply that would compromise her in any way. Furthermore, by her unflinching manner, she completely baffled our celebrated Ulysse Moscati, who was the prosecutor in charge of the interrogation.

He was so surprised at the young girl's comportment that he thought he ought to give a full account to His Holiness, Pope Clement VIII, now fortunately in office.

His Holiness wished to see and study the reports of the trial. He feared lest Judge Moscati, well known for his deep knowledge and superior wisdom, had succumbed to Beatrice's beauty and had spared her during the interrogation. His Holiness therefore transferred the conduct of the trial to a harsher judge. Indeed, this barbarian was ruthless enough to put her beautiful body mercilessly *ad torturam capillorum* – that is to say, that they questioned Beatrice while hanging her by her hair.

The new interrogator had her strung up by the rope and then confronted with her stepmother and brothers. As soon as Giacomo and Signora Lucrezia laid eyes on her, they cried out, 'The crime has been committed. You must repent and not allow your body to be torn apart by your pointless obstinacy.'

'Would you bring shame upon our house then,' replied the girl, 'and die in dishonour? You are very wrong, but if that is what you wish, so be it.'

Turning the the police, she said, 'Untie me and read me my mother's confession. I will admit what should be admitted and I will deny what should be denied.'

This was done. Beatrice confessed all that was true. Immediately the chains were removed from all four and, because she had not seen her brothers for five months, she wished to dine with them, and they all spent a pleasant day together.

But on the following morning they were again separated. The two brothers were sent to Tordinona prison, and the women remained in Savella. When the Holy Father saw the full report containing the confessions of all four, he commanded that they should at once be tied to the tails of wild horses and thus put to death.

All Rome trembled upon learning of this fearful sentence. Many cardinals and princes went to kneel before the pope, begging him to allow the accused to present their defence.

'Did they give their aged father time to present his?' replied the pope indignantly.

At last, as a special favour, he agreed to grant a stay of execution of twenty-five days. At once the leading Roman lawyers set themselves to write about the case, which had so troubled the town and filled it with compassion. On the twenty-fifth day they all appeared together before His Holiness. Nicolò De Angelis spoke first, but scarcely had he read two lines of his defence when Clement VIII interrupted him.

'What,' cried the pope, 'there are men in Rome who would kill their father and then there are lawyers to defend them?'

No one spoke until Farinacci dared open his mouth.

'Most Holy Father,' said he, 'we are not here to defend the crime but to prove, if we can, that one or several of the accused are innocent.'

The pope signalled to him to continue, and Farinacci spoke for three long hours, after which the pope took all of their statements and sent the lawyers away. As they left, Altieri was last in line. Afraid of compromising himself, he fell on his knees and said to the pope, 'I could do no less than appear in this case, since I am the advocate of the poor.'

To which the pope replied, 'We are not surprised at you but at the others.'

The pope did not retire to bed but spent the night reading the lawyers' pleas, assisted in this task by Cardinal di San Marcello. His Holiness seemed so moved that many began to hold out hope for the lives of the accused. To save Giacomo and Bernardo, the lawyers had placed the whole blame on Beatrice. Since it had been proved during the trial that her father had often used force on her in his criminal intents, the lawyers hoped that she would be pardoned for the murder, as she had a legitimate self-defence. Thus, if she, the main author of the crime, were allowed to live, how could her brothers, who had been persuaded by her, be sentenced to death?

After a night given over to his duties as judge, Clement VIII ordered that the accused be taken back to prison and put in solitary confinement. This new turn of events caused great hopes throughout

Rome, where Beatrice was the focus of attention of the whole case. It was said that she had been in love with Monsignor Guerra but had never compromised her virtue in the least degree. Therefore, in the name of justice, such a monstrous crime could not be imputed to her, for this would be to punish her for using her right to defend herself. What would have happened to her if she had consented to her father's advances? Should human justice increase the misery of such a gentle creature, one so deserving of pity and yet so ill used? After so grim a life, during which every sort of mistreatment had been heaped on her before she was even sixteen years old, did she not have the right to some less appalling days? All Rome seemed ranged in her defence. Would she not have been pardoned had she stabbed Francesco Cenci the first time he had attempted his crime?

Pope Clement VIII was kind and merciful. We began to hope that, slightly ashamed of the outburst with which he had interrupted the lawyers' pleas, he would pardon those who had used force to repel force, admittedly, not on the occasion of the first crime but when it had been attempted again. Rome was in a state of high excitement when the pope received news of the violent death of the Marchesa Constanzia Santa Croce. Her son, Paolo Croce, had just murdered his sixty-year-old mother by stabbing her repeatedly with a dagger when she would not agree to his inheriting all her possessions. The report went on to say that Santa Croce had fled and that there was no hope of catching him. Recalling the recent Massini fratricide and distressed by the frequency of these murders of close relatives, the pope found himself unable to grant a pardon. He received the fatal news of Santa Croce on 6 September at the palace of Monte Cavallo, where he was staying so as to be near the church of Santa Maria degli Angeli, in which the following day he was to consecrate a German cardinal as bishop.

At four o'clock on the Friday afternoon the pope summoned Ferrante Taverna, governor of Rome, and spoke to him thus: 'We are turning the Cenci affair over to you, so that justice may be done by your efforts and as quickly as possible.'

The governor returned to his palace greatly troubled by the command he had just received. Hastening to carry out the death sentence at once, he called a meeting to decide upon the method of execution.

On the Saturday morning, 11 September 1599, the leading nobility of Rome, members of the fraternity of the *confortatori*, gathered at the prisons of Corte Savella, where Beatrice and her stepmother were confined, and Tordinona, where Giacomo and Bernardo Cenci were held.

The Roman nobles, who knew what was going on, spent all Friday night into the small hours rushing between the palaces of Monte Cavallo and those of the chief cardinals to try and establish at least that the women should be put to death inside the prison and not on a shameful scaffold and that young Bernardo Cenci, who, at just fifteen, could hardly have been involved in the plot, should be acquitted.

The noble Cardinal Sforza particularly distinguished himself by his zeal on that fateful night, but although a powerful prince he could achieve nothing. Santa Croce's crime was vile, committed as it had been for the sake of money, whereas Beatrice's crime was committed to save her honour.

While these powerful cardinals made vain efforts, Farinacci, our great legal expert, took the risky step of going straight to the pope. Once in the presence of His Holiness, this astonishing man used his skills to appeal to the pope's conscience, and at last, by the strength of his pleas, he wrested Bernardo Cenci's life.

It must have been four o'clock in the morning of Saturday, 11 September, when the pope issued the announcement. All night work had been going on in the square before the bridge of Castel Sant' Angelo in preparation for the cruel tragedy. However, not all the necessary copies of the death sentence were ready until five a.m., so it was six o'clock before the grim news could be announced to the hapless victims, who were sleeping peacefully.

At first, the young girl could not even summon the strength to dress herself. With piercing shrieks she gave in to utter despair.

'Oh God, how is it possible that I must die so suddenly?'

Lucrezia Petroni said nothing but what was seemly. First she prayed on her knees, then she calmly urged her daughter to accompany her to the chapel, so that the two of them might prepare for the great journey from life to death.

These words calmed Beatrice. The moment her stepmother recalled this great soul to her senses, her extravagant transports of despair gave way to complete serenity and composure. From that moment the girl became a mirror of steadfastness that all Rome admired.

She asked for a notary to make her will, and this was granted. She stipulated that her body be buried in San Pietro in Montorio. She left three hundred thousand scudi to the sisters of the Order of the Stigmata of St Francis. This sum was to endow fifty poor girls. Her example so moved Signora Lucrezia that she too made her will and ordered that her body be taken to San Giorgio. She left five hundred thousand scudi in alms to this church and made other pious legacies.

At eight o'clock they made their confession, heard Mass, and received holy communion. But before attending Mass, Signora Beatrice decided that it would not be seemly to appear on the scaffold, before the eyes of the whole populace, in the rich clothes they were wearing. She ordered two dresses, one for herself, the other for her mother. These were to be like nuns' habits, unadorned at breast and shoulder but simply gathered and with wide sleeves. The stepmother's dress was to be made of black calico, and the young girl's of blue taffeta with a long girdle for the waist.

When the dresses were brought, Signora Beatrice, who was on her knees, arose and said to Signora Lucrezia, 'My lady mother, the hour of our Calvary has arrived. We should prepare ourselves. Let us take these clothes and for the last time assist each other to dress.'

A large scaffold had been erected in the square before the Castel Sant' Angelo bridge, with a block and the executioner's axe. At eight o'clock that morning the Company of Misericordia brought its great crucifix to the prison door. Giacomo Cenci came out first.

On the threshold of the prison gates he knelt devoutly and kissed the Holy Wounds of the crucifix. He was followed by Bernardo Cenci, his young brother, who also had his hands bound behind his back and a wooden blindfold over his eyes. The crowd was huge, and there was pandemonium because of a pot of plants that fell out of a window almost on the head of one of the penitents who stood beside the banner with a lighted brand.

All eyes were fixed on the two brothers, when suddenly the Procurator Fiscal of Rome came forward and said, 'Signor Bernardo, Our Lord has granted you your life. Submit to accompany your kin and pray to God for them.'

At the same moment the boy's two *confortatori* took off the little board that covered his eyes. The executioner arranged Giacomo Cenci in the cart and removed his shirt in order to tear his flesh with red-hot pincers. When the executioner came to Bernardo, he verified the signature of the pardon, untied him, removed his manacles, and, as he was shirtless for the flesh tearing, the executioner placed him on the cart and wrapped him in a cloak of gold brocade. (It was said to be the same cloak given to Marzio by Beatrice after the events in the castle of La Petrella.) The immense crowd, which thronged the road and peered from the windows and rooftops, gave out a great gasp. A hushed murmuring sound was heard as the rumour went forth that the child had been pardoned.

The chanting of psalms began, and the procession moved slowly off through Piazza Navona towards Savella prison. When it arrived at the prison gates the standard halted, the two women came out, made their obeisance to the foot of the Holy Cross and then set out walking, one behind the other. They were dressed as I have described, their heads covered with long taffeta veils that reached to their girdles.

Signora Lucrezia, being a widow, wore a black veil and black velvet slippers without heels, according to custom. The young girl's veil was of blue taffeta, like her dress. She also wore a long cloak of silver brocade that fell from her shoulders, a violet skirt, and white velvet slippers elegantly laced with crimson cords. Dressed thus, she walked with superb grace, and tears rose to everyone's eyes as they watched her coming slowly along in the last rows of the procession.

The hands of both women were free, although their arms were bound to their bodies, so that each could carry a crucifix. These they held firmly before their eyes. The sleeves of their dresses were very wide and their arms could be seen tightly covered to the wrist, as is the fashion in this country.

Signora Lucrezia, who was less resolute, wept continually, while young Beatrice showed great courage. Each time the procession passed a church, she turned her head and genuflected for an instant, saying in a steady voice, '*Adoramus te, Christe.*'

All this time poor Giacomo Cenci was being torn with pincers on the cart, and he too showed great courage.

The procession could barely cross the end of the square in front of the bridge of Castel Sant' Angelo so great were the number of carriages and the throng of people. The women were led straight into the chapel which had been prepared for them, and Giacomo was taken in after them.

Young Bernardo, covered by the brocaded cloak,

was led directly to the scaffold, so that everyone thought he had not been pardoned and was to die. So overcome by fear was the poor child that he fainted at the second step he took up the scaffold. He was revived with cold water and made to sit opposite the executioner's axe.

The executioner went to fetch Lucrezia Petroni. Her hands were now bound behind her back, the veil was no longer over her shoulders. She appeared in the square accompanied by the banner, her head swathed in the black taffeta veil. There she made her peace with God and kissed His Holy Wounds. She was told to leave her slippers on the pavement. When she stood on the scaffold and the black taffeta veil was removed, she was humiliated at being seen with breast and shoulders exposed. She looked down at herself, then at the axe, and gave a slight shrug of resignation. Tears came to her eyes, and she said, 'Oh God, and you my brethren, pray for my soul.'

Not knowing what she had to do, she asked Alessandro, the first executioner, how she should position herself. He told her to sit astride the beam of the executioner's block. But this movement seemed to offend her modesty, and it took her a long time to manage it. The following description is acceptable to the Italian public, who insist upon knowing every last detail. The modesty of this lady was such that she injured her breast. The executioner showed the head to the people and then wrapped it in the black taffeta veil.

While the axe was being prepared for the young girl, a scaffolding loaded with onlookers collapsed, and a number of people were killed. Thus they appeared in God's presence before Beatrice.

When Beatrice saw the banner return to the chapel to fetch her, she asked animatedly, 'Is Madam my mother dead?'

They told her she was. Beatrice fell to her knees before the crucifix and prayed fervently for her mother's soul. Then she spoke aloud and at length to the crucifix.

'Lord God, Thou returnest for me and willingly I follow Thee, not despairing of Thy mercy for my great sin', etc.

She then recited several psalms and prayers in praise of God. When at last the executioner stood before her, with a rope, she said, 'Bind this body, which must be punished, and free this soul, which shall go forth to immortality and eternal glory.'

She then rose, said a prayer, left her slippers at the foot of the steps, and climbed up onto the scaffold. Nimbly she threw her leg over the beam, placed her neck where the axe would fall, and arranged herself perfectly on her own so as to avoid being touched by the executioner. So swiftly did she move that she prevented her shoulders and breast from being exposed to the public when the taffeta veil was removed. The stroke was a long time in coming because there was a delay. All this time she called aloud the name of Jesus Christ and the Most Holy Virgin.

The body jerked violently at the moment of death. Poor Bernardo Cenci, who was still seated on the scaffold, fainted once again, and it took his *confortatori* a half-hour to revive him. Then Giacomo Cenci appeared on the scaffold. Here we must pass over the hideous details. Giacomo Cenci was bludgeoned to death.

Bernardo was at once taken back to prison. He had a high fever, and they bled him. As for the unfortunate women, each was laid out in a coffin and set down a little way from the scaffold by the statue of St Paul, which is the first on the right-hand side of the bridge of Sant' Angelo. They remained there until a quarter past four in the afternoon. Around each bier burned four candles of white wax.

Then, with the remains of Giacomo Cenci, they were taken to the palazzo of the consul of Florence. At a quarter past nine in the evening, the body of the young girl, clothed once more in her own garments and crowned with a wreath of flowers, was carried to San Pietro in Montorio. She looked ravishingly beautiful and seemed to be asleep. She was buried before the high altar and the *Transfiguration* by Raphael of Urbino. Her body was accompanied by fifty great lighted candles and all the Franciscan monks and nuns in Rome.

Lucrezia Petroni was taken at ten o'clock in the evening to the church of San Giorgio. During this tragic drama the crowd was enormous. As far as the eye could see, the streets were full of carriages and people. Scaffolding, windows, and roofs were crowded with onlookers. The sun was so hot that day that many people fainted. Large numbers fell into a fever, and, by the time all was over at a quarter to two and the crowd dispersed, many had been suffocated, others trampled by horses. The number of dead was considerable.

Signora Lucrezia Petroni was rather short than tall, and though fifty years old she was still well formed. She had fine features, a small nose, black eyes, and a pale face with a luminous complexion. She had wispy chestnut hair.

Beatrice Cenci, who was to inspire eternal compassion, was just sixteen years old. She was small and curvaceous, with a pretty face and dimples in her cheeks, so that when dead and crowned with flowers one would have said she was asleep and even that she was laughing, as she often did when alive. She had a small mouth, fair hair, and natural curls. As she went to her death, her fair curls fell over her eyes, which, adding a certain poignancy, aroused compassion.

Giacomo Cenci was small and plump, with a pale face and black beard. He was nearly twenty-six when he died. Bernardo Cenci looked exactly like his sister, and, since he wore his hair long as she did, when he appeared on the scaffold many took him for his sister.

The sun was so hot that a number of the spectators died in the night, amongst them Ubaldino Ubaldini, a young man of unusual beauty, who had previously enjoyed perfect health. He was the brother of Signor Renzi, a well-known Roman. Thus the shades of the Cenci departed in good company.

Yesterday, Tuesday, 14 September, on the occasion of the feast of the Holy Cross, the penitents of San Marcello made use of their privilege to free Signor Bernardo Cenci from prison. He had to pay, within a year, four hundred thousand scudi to the Most Holy Trinity of Ponte Sisto.

Added by another hand

The present-day Francesco and Bernardo Cenci are the descendants of the aforesaid Bernardo Cenci.

The noted Farinacci, who, by his doggedness, saved the life of young Cenci, has published his defence pleas. He gives only one extract from plea no. 66, which he delivered to Clement VIII on behalf of the Cenci family. This defence, which is in Latin, would take up six long pages and it is to my deep regret that I cannot include it here, as it shows how people thought in 1599 and is full of good sense. Many years after 1599, Farinacci, when sending his defence speeches to the printers, added this note to what he had said on behalf of the Cenci: *Omnes fuerunt ultimo supplicio effecti, excepto Bernardo qui ad triremes cum bonorum confiscatione condemnatus fuit, ac etiam ad interessendum aliorum morti prout interfuit.** The end of this Latin note is touching, but I suppose the reader is tired of so long a tale.

* All parties suffered the final punishment, except for Bernardo, who was condemned to the galleys, with the confiscation of his possessions, and so he too partook in the deaths of the others.

Appendixes

I

Background Notes

A. The Geopolitical Terrain

Sixteenth-century Italy was – as Italy had been for hundreds of years previously and would continue to be for hundreds of years into the future – a patchwork and kaleidoscope of states, many of them of minor importance, some independent, some under foreign domination. Cheek by jowl were bickering and warring duchies and republics, principalities and kingdoms. The two largest powers were the Papal States, which ran north from Rome through to Ancona on the Adriatic, and the Kingdom of Naples, which occupied the whole of the south of the Italian peninsula and was ruled by Spain. There were colourful anomalies. In 1551, in the endless power shifts, a principality of Parma was carved out of Milan as a reward for papal co-operation. Transferred to the pope's family as a personal fiefdom, it never became part of the papal territory.

Of this turbulent time, the historian Janet Penrose Trevelyan has written:

Rome under Paul IV assumed the air of a 'well-behaved religious community.' But in reality [the Papacy] had but added the sin of hypocrisy to their former sins of violence and dissolute living, and beneath the pious aspect of Rome the corruption of morals and of all ordinary standards of integrity was as profound as ever. In Rome, more than in any other Italian state, the venality of justice became part of the recognized financial system; all but the very highest Judgeships were bought and sold like any other venal office of the Curia . . . The people, whether high or low, seldom voluntarily resorted to the courts of justice, but continued to carry on their private feuds and assassinations in their own fashion – the nobles by hiring professional murderers, or 'bravi,' to whom they gave the protection of their palaces, the peasants by organizing themselves in roving bands of brigands . . .

For centuries Italy had been a fragmented land enmeshed in the power struggles that raged between the French, Spaniards, Germans, and the Papal States. There was no central or national guidance. The separateness of the small northern republics and city-states was exaggerated, and Italy bled in battles between the secular and spiritual masters of Europe. To a greater or lesser degree, the endless, unbridgeable division was that which harked back to the Guelphs, the faction supporting the pope, and the Ghibellines, the faction supporting the Holy Roman Emperor. To complicate matters, even these allegiances were known periodically to shift from one group to the other. Meanwhile, as Stendhal's Roman tales reflect and portray, the whole peninsula was riddled with chaos, turmoil, lawlessness, and corruption of every grade.

B. Stendhal's Popes

The following list of chiefly sixteenth-century popes is taken from an appendix to Stendhal's *Promenades dans Rome* (1829). A number of these popes figure in the years covered by the three stories of the present book. In his entry on Gregory XIV, Stendhal has committed two errors. The pope's correct surname is Sfondrati, and the Como villa is Sfondati. The two are unrelated.

Paul IV, *Carafa*, Neapolitan, elected in 1555, reigned 4 years, 2 months, and 27 days. An angry old man, but of good faith, he thought nothing of stamping out heresy by torture; decline of the arts.

Pius IV, of the *Medici* of Milan, elected in 1559, reigned 3 years, 11 months, and 15 days.

St Pius V, *Ghislieri*, was Grand Inquisitor when he was elected in 1566. Governed the Church for 6 years and 24 days. His bloodthirsty zeal made him a saint. See his letters, published by M. de Potter.

Gregory XIII, *Buoncompagni*, from Bologna, elected in 1572, governed the Church for 12 years, 10 months, and 28 days. He rejoiced at the St Bartholomew's Day massacre [in Paris]. See the Vatican frescoes.

Sixtus V, *Peretti*. This great prince was born under thatch, in the village of Grottamare, in Le Marche. Elected in 1585, he only governed the Church for 5 years, 4 months, and 3 days. This short reign was enough for him to fill Rome with monuments and to stamp out brigandage. He gave the court of Rome statutes that could be considered a kind of constitution. For example, he fixed the number of cardinals at seventy, and tried to ensure that four of these gentlemen were always chosen from among monks.

Urban VII, *Castagna*, Roman, only reigned 13 days, elected in 1590.

Gregory XIV, *Sfrondati*, from Milan, elected in 1590, reigned for 10 months and 10 days. See the beautiful Villa Sfrondati, one of the world's loveliest places, on the shores of Lake Como.

Innocent IX, *Facchinetti*, from Bologna, elected in 1591, reigned for a little more than 2 months.

Clement VIII, *Aldobrandini*, from Fano, elected in 1592, reigned for 13 years, 1 month, and 3 days.

You will remember the beautiful Villa Aldobrandini, in Frascati.

Leo XI, *Medici*, from Florence, elected in 1605, reigned only 27 days.

Paul V, *Borghese*, Roman, elected in 1605, reigned for 15 years, 8 months, and 13 days. He finished St Peter's, whose shape he changed by adding the three chapels closest to the entrance. He left immense wealth to his family, who became French.

C. Stendhal and Money

In his autobiography, *The Life of Henry Brulard* (ch. VII), Stendhal recalls that 'money was, quite understandably, my father's great concern, whereas I have never thought about it without disgust. The very idea of money suggests cruel suffering to me, since having money gives me no pleasure, whereas the lack of it is a hateful misfortune.' Two pages on, he continues: 'Any attention paid to money matters was considered supremely vile and base in my family. It was somehow indecent to talk about money; money was like some distressing necessity of life, unfortunately indispensable, like the privy, but which must never be spoken of.' And two paragraphs on: 'This reluctance to talk about money, so contrary to Parisian custom, came from goodness knows where and has become completely ingrained in my character.'

Ingrained in Stendhal's character, perhaps, but certainly not in his writings. Salaries, stipends, incomes, the cost or monetary value of things are constantly brought to our attention throughout his novels and stories. The French 'love money above all things', he informs us, and *The Red and the Black*, the first of Stendhal's two masterworks, is crammed with details of land values, salaries, the costs of a tutor, priests' stipends, private incomes, and so forth. *The Charterhouse of Parma*, the second of his great novels, likewise: the amount of a dowry, how to live in Milan on a pension of only 1,500 francs, the 80,000-franc cost of building an embankment, diamonds for conversion into cash, the price of buying and swapping warhorses, the stipends of high-ranking officials at the court of Parma, the price paid for a Canova bust of Napoleon, the earnings of an actress, and so on and so on.

The Abbess of Castro, charting the love affair of a poor young peasant and the daughter of the district's richest man, provides fertile ground for money matters, which play a considerable role in the story. The daughter's family is lavish in its contributions to Church and clergy: a silver altar lamp worth several hundred scudi; a thousand piastres that her father gave the friars for fetching his son's body from a battle-field; a ring worth a thousand piastres for a *fratone's* favour; a hefty bribe of two hundred thousand piastres in land or in money to have the daughter made abbess of her convent.

So assiduous is Stendhal in his accounting that at one point in the story 'The Cenci' he records that Francesco Cenci had inherited 'a net income of a hundred and sixty thousand scudi (around 2,500,000 francs of 1837)'. In a note in the margins of the Italian manuscript (dated 15 May 1833), Stendhal adds: 'An income of 550,000 francs in about 1550. By how much should this sum be multiplied to find the equivalent in 1833? I think it should be multiplied by four. Francesco Cenci would today have an income of 2,200,000 francs. We note that he evaded a prosecution for sodomy at a cost of 1,100,000 francs (or 4,400,000 francs now). The rich today are fined nowhere near so much.' Elsewhere, in a note to the story 'Victoria Accoramboni', Stendhal reckons the multiplier should be five.

Dickens records (1845) that ten scudi equalled about £2 2s 6d.

In his 1969 edition of *The Red and the Black* (titled *Red and Black*) the American scholar Robert M. Adams probes at length the complex issue of money. In the 1830s the franc was 'equal in English currency to about one shilling thruppence'. Adams calculates that 'To get contemporary (1968) equivalents, we had better try multiplying by ten.' But he warns that multiplying by ten can defy credibility, for 'It is apparent that Stendhal . . . is given to exaggerating the extremes. His rich are immensely rich, his poor are poor to the point of squalor, and the contrast between them is a theme of his art.'

In his biography of Stendhal, Robert Alter has reckoned, with caveats, that 'one franc during [Stendhal's time] might more or less equal two 1979 U.S. dollars or one 1979 English pound.'

There are other complications. Stendhal resorted to a range of French and other monetary units: the franc, sou, livre, écu, napoleon, piastre, and louis. In his Italian stories he translates Italian coinage into French equivalents. Thus the Italian scudo becomes interchangeable with piastres or francs or écus. The English translations of Stendhal compound matters, and in them we find additional units such as ducats, crowns, florins, doubloons, sequins, and so forth.

In the current translation of these stories, aiming for simplicity and verisimilitude, Susan Ashe has resorted to the usage of the Italian originals. Except in two instances, where Spanish coinage reflects the reality of the day in the Aragonese-controlled Kingdom of Naples, she employs only terms of Italian currency – that is, scudi, *baiocchi*, and *zecchini*.

2

Brigands in Italy
by Stendhal

These pages were originally destined for Stendhal's *Rome, Naples et Florence* (1826), an enlarged edition of his previous *Rome, Naples et Florence en 1817*. Owing to a publisher's oversight, however, his account of Italian brigands, along with some other Italian pieces, was omitted from the book. Presented by the author to his cousin Romain Colomb, this supplementary material was included in Colomb's own *Journal d'un voyage en Italie et en Suisse pendant l'année 1828*, from which Stendhal scholars have subsequently identified it and winkled it out. 'Les Brigands en Italie' now appears as an appendix in the Pleiade edition of Stendhal's *Voyages en Italie*. The following translation by Susan Ashe may well be the first time these pages appear in English.

In France and in most European states, we are in general agreement as to what we call those men whose profession is to hold to ransom travellers on the highroads. They are brigands. In Italy, they are rightly called murderers, thieves, bandits, and outlaws, but it would be a great mistake to think that their activities are regarded in that country with such vehement, all-round condemnation as they receive elsewhere.

Everyone fears brigands, but the odd thing is that as individuals we feel sorry for them when they are punished for their crimes. Indeed, we nurse a kind of respect for them even when they exercise the appalling right they have assumed for themselves.

In Italy, the common people enjoy reading little poems that describe in detail the remarkable lives of the most famous bandits. Anything heroic delights this public, and their admiration for such men has much of the love that in antiquity the Greeks felt for certain of their demi-gods.

In 1580, in central Lombardy, a formidable body of assassins arose. They were known as *bravi*. Many a great lord had one such troop of men at his disposal and deployed them mainly to satisfy his whims, whether involving hatred, revenge, or even love. With unequalled daring and skill, the *bravi* carried out hazardous missions and left everyone, including the authorities, in fear and trembling. After 1583, the Spanish governor of Milan made vain attempts to eradicate these dangerous syndicates. He promulgated edict after edict, none of which prevented the *bravi* from gaining recruits. In 1628 these men were thriving and had gained a terrifying reputation for murder and abduction.

The *bravi* were used by their masters to serve as seconds in any of their duels. Blind obedience, silence, and shrewdness were the chief qualities of the *bravo*'s trade.

Brigandage has existed in Italy from time immemorial, but it was towards the middle of the sixteenth century that it began to enjoy considerable expansion. Most of those who took up this way of life were men who found it more honourable to keep their independence than to bend the knee to papal authority. The memory of the medieval republics still troubled everyone. In a word, the end seemed to justify the means. What gave these men their savage energy was an urge to resist the government rather than to make a premeditated attack on the fortunes or lives of private individuals. Alfonso Piccolomini, Duke of Montemariano, and Marco Sciarra successfully commanded bands of brigands against the armies of the pope.

Piccolomini travelled to France in 1583, where he served in the army and stayed on for eight years. On 16 March 1591, Ferdinand, Grand Duke of Tuscany, hanged him, despite the pleas of Philippe II and of Gregory XIV, in whose countries he had spread destruction. Piccolomini's small force was made up of all the criminals of Tuscany, Romagna, the Marche, and the Papal States.

Sciarra was the chieftain of a large band of formidable warriors, who, under Gregory XIII towards the end of the sixteenth century, ravaged the Papal States and the borders of Tuscany and Naples. This army could sometimes muster several thousand men. Sixtus V managed to keep them away from Rome but not to tame them. Clement VIII attacked Sciarra so fiercely in 1592 that the notorious brigand was forced to renounce his deadly trade and to go into service with the Venetian Republic, accompanied by five hundred of his boldest companions. He was sent to Dalmatia to fight against the Croatian pirates, but Clement complained vociferously that these brigands, whom he was pursuing, were thereby removed from his jurisdiction, and he asked for them to be delivered up. The Venetian senate took fright, had Sciarra assassinated, and sent his troops to die of the plague in Crete.

Forced into endless struggles with papal forces, the brigands took refuge in the forests, where, lacking all resources, they stole and killed to stay alive. Their sphere of operation became the mountains that run from Ancona to Terracina and from Ravenna to Naples. But lack of means to suppress them or a failure of will on the part of governments turned into a kind of tacit sanction, and brigandage soon spread throughout Italy. Its independent, adventurous lifestyle lured a number of courageous men who, if properly guided, might have been capable of great things. To take to the forest was often the only means whereby someone suffering persecution could avenge himself for the wrongs of a great lord or a powerful abbot.

The Colonna and Orsini clans owned nearly all the lands around Rome. These two powerful families had been enemies for almost two centuries. In setting up a bitter war, in seeking to destroy each other, they completed the devastation of the Roman plain that the barbarians had so successfully begun, reducing it to the emptiness and insalubrity in which we now find it. All the nobility, under orders of the redoubtable condottieri, belonged either to the Colonna faction or to that of the Orsini. Sixtus V managed to reconcile them by attaching them to himself in order to ensure his authority. This pope, an intelligent man with a good head, had two young nieces. He married one to the eldest Colonna son and the other to the eldest son of the Orsini. The rivalry between the two families dated from the pontificate of Boniface VIII (1294), for whom the Orsini had procured the tiara.

The whole of Italy was infested by brigands, but it was mainly in the Papal States and the Kingdom of Naples that they held sway for the longest time and where they operated in the most constant and methodical way. There they had an organization, privileges, and a guarantee of impunity. If they became strong enough to intimidate governments, their fortune was made. It was therefore towards this goal that they constantly aimed throughout the period during which they plied their infamous trade. A man felt he was back in the days of the barbarians when, in the absence of any law, force was the only arbiter, the only recognized power. What kind of government is it that can be reduced to trembling before a handful of criminals! Twenty or thirty men could spread terror throughout a country and force all the pope's troops into battle.

The city of Brescia and its surroundings were notorious at the time for having the greatest number of assassinations – roughly two hundred a year. These days French military police and Austrian bayonets have put a stop to this state of affairs.

In Calabria the struggle that the French kept up for ten years (1797 to 1808) will long be remembered. Encouraged by the English, the brigands were at first the core of the royalist uprising. Later, some malcontents, prompted by religious fanaticism or by pure patriotism, joined them. Perhaps never has resistance to a foreign yoke been accompanied by such a frenzy of bloodshed. Both sides fought a battle to the death. All the horror, all the brutality, of a civil war drenched this wretched country in gore. The band of assassins led by Francatrippa was supplied by Sicilian brigands, whom the English frequently landed on the coasts (1807).

It is fairly common in Calabria for the family of someone who has committed a murder to offer to treat with the family of the victim. If the price demanded is so high that an agreement cannot or will not be reached and the complaint is brought to law, an irreconcilable hatred arises between the two families, and a long series of revenge attacks may be expected. Calabrian peasants still speak with pride of their ancestors and of Skanderbeg, who, in 1443, raised the banner of independence against Sultan Amurath, the usurper of Skanderbeg's estates and the murderer of his family.

Stripped of all civil and political rights, delivered up to the tender mercies of an arbitrary self-proclaimed divinity, the subjects of St Peter must also be held to ransom or massacred by brigands who infest the Church's domains.

It has to be said that the government by its pusillanimous conduct and cowardly condoning of the murderers – by the absolutions, rewards, remittances, even employment with which it gratifies them – makes itself complicit. What more could it do if it wanted to encourage them? One pope consigned all decency to oblivion by knighting Ghino di Tacco, a well-known thief, simply because he admired the outlaw's courage.

These brigands bore no resemblance to common thieves. As I have said, it was not always need that launched them on a criminal career. Often it was chance, idleness, or a natural predilection, but how many of them would never have become brigands had they had land to cultivate?

Those who aspired to join submitted to a period of severe testing. Many owned a house, cattle, and were married. They obeyed a chief whose power was absolute. But freely chosen, this chief could himself be deposed and even put to death should he betray his companions or break the rules.

The bandits wear a kind of uniform. Their picturesque garb is somewhat military: shortish trousers in blue cloth, with big silver loops on their scarlet garters; a waistcoat of the same cloth, adorned by parallel rows of silver buttons; a short, cutaway jacket, also of blue cloth, eqipped with pockets on either side; a brown cloak thrown over the shoulder; open shirt with turned-down collar; a tall, pointed red felt hat, with cords or ribbons of different colours; stockings held up by narrow leather bands, which go into sandals or tight ankle boots; a wide leather cartridge belt fastened by a silver buckle; a knapsack; a shoulder belt with a sabre hanging from it; a fork, a spoon, a dagger; and round their necks is a red ribbon, to which is attached a silver heart that lies on the chest. They wear ex-votos under their clothes and display on the outside a medallion of the Virgin and the baby Jesus. This is the military and religious dress of these men who, slaves to a strict discipline, march only in largish bands. They pay their spies and suppliers well and are rarely betrayed.

Their somewhat nomadic life is divided between the care of flocks of goats, on which they partly subsist, and the surveillance of high roads or byways, where they lie in wait for travellers. Often these bandit hordes are simply villagers from the Sabine or Abruzzi hills. For part of the year they work in the fields, but as their toil in this rocky terrain does not meet the needs of their families, they give in to their natural bent for murder and pillage. The brigand's life means no more to them than an existence that they are fully aware carries the risk of the scaffold. As most of the population is enrolled under the banner of a handful of chieftains, these men always have at their behest a small army as promptly mustered as they are dispersed after an action.

On their expeditions the bandits are usually assisted by shepherds. The men who take up shepherding lead a half-savage existence. While this allows them links with towns where they can obtain provisions, it cuts them off sufficiently from social ties to render them indifferent to the crimes of others.

Confronting dangers, suffering privations, enduring exhaustion shapes the everyday life of brigands. Most often they sleep in the depths of a ravine, wrapped in their coats, shelterless but for the vault of the sky. From there these land pirates hunt down their victims, carry them off to their dens, and butcher them if they cannot pay the fixed ransom. This is the treatment meted out to local people. Strangers are normally only stripped, but sometimes left naked where they were attacked. The bandits' first command to travellers whom they are robbing is to keep their eyes on the ground.

Often a band unexpectedly comes on a flock of sheep. Then, if their hunger is whetted, the thieves order the shepherds to slaughter one or more animals. The sheep are skinned on the spot, cut into pieces that are grilled on the end of a gun barrel, and devoured. Bread and wine appear by similar means. During the meal the brigands generally force the shepherds, whose flock they are decimating, to chop firewood and draw water, etc., etc.

When a band settles somewhere, it takes all the precautions that a small army adopts in hostile country. Sentries, relieved at short intervals, are posted at various points where a surprise attack might occur. Once these measures have been taken, the bandits separate into groups, some playing cards, others playing *morra*. Still others dance or listen to a tale or a song in carefree and complete safety.

In the course of such an adventurous life, the two things that comfort the Italian brigand and that he never lays aside are his gun for defending his life and his medallion of the Virgin for saving his soul. Nothing is more terrifying than this blend of ferocity and superstition. The outlaw is convinced that death on the scaffold, preceded by a priest's absolution, will assure him a place in heaven. Often a similar belief impels a wretch to commit some crime that will incur capital punishment, the better to be assured of the happiness that the sacrifice of his life will render certain. Last of all, they will assassinate you in style, rosary and chaplet in hand, the stiletto thrust accompanied by a 'for the love of God'.

A bandit, accused of several murders, appears before his judges. Far from denying the crimes imputed to him, he admits others until then unknown to the law; but when someone asks if he observed the fast day, the devout rascal grows angry and is mortally offended. 'Are you accusing me of not being a good Christian?' he says bitterly to the interrogating magistrate.

A worthy Christian, Signor Tambroni, confirms that there were eighteen thousand murders in the Papal States during the reign of Pius VI (from 1775 to 1799). There were ten thousand, of which four thousand took place in Rome alone, under Clement XIII. It is known that during the pontificate of Pius VII a large number of bandits achieved fame.

A certain Maino from Spinetta, near Alessandria, was one of the most remarkable men of his century. He gave himself the title Emperor of the Alps and under this designation he signed proclamations that he posted along the road. On State occasions, when he reviewed his troops, he would appear in the uniforms and decorations he had stripped from generals and high-ranking French civil servants. Maino fought for many years against the French gendarmerie. Finally, betrayed by a woman in whose house he was staying in the village of Spinetta, where he was born, he was suddenly surrounded by police and two brigades of gendarmes. A fierce battle took place between this one individual and a troop of men armed to the teeth. The hero of the highroads defended himself like a lion, killed several of his adversaries, and did not flee his refuge until it was set afire. He escaped, climbed a wall, took a bullet, which broke his thigh, and was finally killed on the spot still fighting the gendarmes. Maino was only twenty-five years old.

Such a man will succumb under the all-out efforts of a well-organized military police. He will pay on the scaffold for his crimes and his daring, but opinion will ascribe more shrewdness to him than to many generals who have made reputations for themselves.

Parella, whose appalling crimes spread terror throughout the Kingdom of Naples, was hunted by French soldiers for three years. Unable to capture him, the minister, Salicetti, put a price on Parella's head. One day, a peasant, a barber, the brigand's servant and confidant of two years, tried to lodge a complaint against him. Succumbing to the lure of profit and to a desire for revenge, he slit his master's throat with his razor, handed in the head, and received four hundred ducats as the reward for this act.

The chieftain known as Diecinove, because one of his toes was missing, was corrupted by blood even more than by gold. Before killing his victims he would slowly torture them with barbaric pleasure. Having exhausted rather than satisfied his brutality,

Diecinove proposed an amnesty with the papal government, which was accepted.

Once pardoned as bandits and absolved as Christians, Diecinove and his companions could present themselves with impunity to the relatives of those they had butchered. After sitting at their table and taking part in family meals, these thugs, on leaving, would demand more silver in return for the consideration they claimed to have given when practising their trade as thieves. No one dared refuse. In this way, without running the slightest risk, they retained the benefits of their former profession.

Corampono's band, having exceeded Diecinove's in brutality, obtained the same immunity.

From Terracina to Fondi, from Fondi to Itri, is classic brigand territory, the native land of the notorious Giuseppe Mastrilli. Love made a murderer of him. He was banished from the Papal States and the Kingdom of Naples, returned there several times, always escaped justice, and died peacefully, declaring repentance for his crimes. Before becoming chief of his band, this adroit character had belonged to old Barba Girolamo's troop.

Mastrilli played an important role in one of the strangest counter-revolutionary parades Europe has seen since 1789. This brigand was to be hanged for his crimes in Montalbano, a small town near the toe of the Italian boot, when Cardinal Ruffo, general of the Calabrian royalist peasantry and the only intelligent man on the monarchist side, judged it useful to the cause of Ferdinand IV to present Mastrilli to his soldiers and the people as the Duke of Calabria, whom he resembled. The bandit appeared on a balcony, decked out with the Orders of St Ferdinand and the Golden Fleece. Fooled by this display, the crowd erupted into cheers and welcomed him with the greatest enthusiasm. The prince of the moment presented his hand to Cardinal Ruffo, and His Eminence kissed it with profound respect.

Before assuming command of the little troop that obeyed Ruffo, Mastrilli took the precaution of assuring himself of immunity and a financial reward from the legitimate king. Supported by the people he had just abused with such impudence, our hero was able to assume a tone of authority and dictate his conditions to the cardinal.

The name Mastrilli had already been made famous towards the middle of the last century by an earlier brigand. The crimes this man committed and the skill with which he evaded justice, made him so dangerous that a price had to be put on his head. He was betrayed and killed while out hunting. In 1766 you could see his head displayed on the gates of Terracina, near Naples.

All Italy trembled in 1806 at the very name of Fra Diavolo. Born in Itri, this brigand spread terror mainly along the Mediterranean coast, confining his activities to the Papal States and the Kingdom of Naples. The sun-blackened former monk and ex-convict, killed his fellow brigands by taste and out of need, sometimes saving them on a whim or helping them out of kindness. In all he did, he was devoted to the Virgin and the saints. After a life of brigandage he went on to become a counter-revolutionary, rising to the rank of a senior officer in the army of Cardinal Ruffo and cutting throats in Naples out of a sense of duty to the altar and the throne. He was always covered in amulets and armed with daggers. After many deeds of astonishing boldness and courage, Fra Diavolo fell captive to a French detachment. He was tried and hanged.

A band with headquarters in the neighbourhood of Sonnino spread terror from Fondi to Rome. Its chiefs, Mazochi and Garbarone, were gifted with a hellish genius. The plan they conceived to carry the pupils of the seminary of Terracina off to their mountain fastness was truly unbelievable.

The worthy cleric in charge of the seminary pondered at length on a way to put an end to the appalling crimes that the brigands were committing. One day, spurred by enthusiasm, he put his crucifix on his back, climbed to the bandits' mountain lair, marched into the troop and planted in their midst the symbol of redemption. This devout missionary recalled to the bandits in vivid terms the evils they were spreading throughout the country. He begged them to abandon their murderous trade and persuaded them to give up whatever they had obtained by pillage and murder. In other words, he said all the most convincing things inspired by his apostolic philanthropy. Bit by bit, the brigands seemed moved. They accepted the cleric's suggestions. Confessing their crimes, they even declared their sincere repentance and desire to return to the bosom of the Church. The elderly priest wept tears of joy and suggested that the thieves prove their good intentions by accompanying him to his seminary. They followed him there, listened to his precepts, took part in all the prayers, and, in a word, fulfilled all the duties of good Christians.

Every day the good churchman thanked God for the happy conversion that had brought peace to the countryside. The sincerity of his new converts was beyond suspicion. Obliged to be away for a short while, the priest left for Velletri, having made his fond farewells. Each man kissed his hand, and the worthy cleric crossed the Pontine marshes, pleasantly dwelling on the gentle thoughts that accompany a kind deed.

As soon as the priest had left the new converts, they began to set in motion the bold plan that they had so cleverly prepared. That very night, the scoundrels took all the seminarists off to their mountain retreat. There the students, prompted by daggers at their hearts, wrote letters inviting their relatives to remit at once a given sum for their ransom.

By the time the period assigned for the arrival of these tributes expired, three of the luckless young men had not been ransomed. Two had their throats cut, and a third, about to suffer the same fate, threw himself at the feet of the assassins, calling on St Anthony. This saved him, and he was sent back to his family with a safe conduct.

In 1813, after a five-year-long pursuit, the French police managed to lay hands on the powerful chieftain known as the Calabrian. To ennoble himself, the man took on political airs and tried to become known as the head of a Roman peasant revolt. He awarded himself the most pompous titles.

Aggrieved by his arrest and desperate to prevent his execution, the Calabrian's band sent a spokesman to the officer of the gendarmes. The brigands offered, for thirty sous a day, to take charge of protecting the road across the Pontine marshes from other bandits. In return, the authorities agreed not to try the Calabrian and deported him to Corsica. This strange treaty concluded, each of the parties religiously observed its terms.

The band known as Independence – commanded, I believe, by De Cesaris – reigned over Calabria in 1817 with absolute and terrible power. The group consisted of thirty men and four women. Landowners and farmers were the main tribute payers. They took pains not to fail to place on a certain day at a certain hour at the foot of a tree or the base of a column, whatever was demanded of them. One farmer however wanted to rid himself of this heavy burden. Instead of bringing his tribute, he tipped off the authorities, and troops on foot and on horseback surrounded the Independents. Finding themselves tricked, the brigands shot their way out, leaving the field covered with the bodies of their enemies. Three days later, they took the most terrible revenge on the ill-fated farmer. Having tortured him and condemned him to death, they threw him into a huge cauldron in which milk was boiled to make cheese. The bandits then forced each of his servants to eat a piece of their master's body.

During the famine of 1817, the chief of the Independents distributed goods to the poor on behalf of the rich. The ration was one and a half pounds of bread for a man, one pound for a woman, and twice as much if she were pregnant.

In 1819 a most enterprising band was encamped near Tivoli. One day they abducted the archpriest of Vicovaro after killing his nephew, who had tried to defend himself. The ransom for the priest and one of his companions in distress was so high it could not be paid, so the brigands sent the ears of the captives and, later, one of their fingers to their families. In the end, tired of waiting – or perhaps fed up with the moaning of the unfortunate hostages, the bandits butchered them.

In January 1825 Mr Hunt, a young Englishman recently married to a very pretty wife, arrived in Naples.

He visited the antiquities of Paestum accompanied by numerous servants, who served him dinner in the temple of Neptune. Unfortunately the servants had brought along some dishes and other articles of silver plate; in addition, the wife wore valuable rings. After a few hours, the Englishman left with his entourage. Two hundred yards from Paestum he was held up by peasants, who demanded everything he had in his carriage, but expressed themselves with a certain reassuring urbanity. Mr Hunt took the affair with good humour and laughingly threw them the fruit which had been the dessert. As he leaned down to pick up some that had fallen to the floor of the carriage, the peasants thought he was looking for a weapon. They fired point blank. One bullet passed through the husband's body and struck his wife. They were driven several miles from the sad scene. The husband expired two hours later and the wife the next day.

If the deceased had been ordinary people the affair would have had no repercussions, but as they came from a high-ranking family the English ambassador insisted that the murderers be arrested. He held to this, and the peasants were tried and executed.

The chieftain Mezzapinta, having fallen into the hands of the carabinieri, was imprisoned in the Castel Sant' Angelo with twenty-seven of his men on 1 November 1825. An honest young priest had had them captured. The brigands were surrounded by the pope's troops on one of the wildest mountains in the Abruzzi, on the borders of the Papal States. They had little chance of escape. With great patience, the saintly priest befriended them and, promising the Holy Father's absolution, he gently led them, one by one, to a colonel of the gendarmerie, who was lying in ambush with his regiment a few miles away. Those who admired the priest's behaviour thought he should be rewarded with a bishopric. I do not know if he was given one.

Gasparoni, at present in a Roman prison, commanded a band of some two hundred men. He was hunted down as the perpetrator of one hundred and forty-three murders. His first crime was committed when at the age of sixteen he murdered his parish priest, who, strangely enough, had refused him absolution for a theft. At the age of eighteen, Gasparoni distinguished himself in a battle against the army, killing or wounding twenty people. By this stroke of genius he gained command of the band in which he served.

Among this troop's memorable deeds, the abduction of nuns from the convent of Monte Commodo should be mentioned. Thirty-four young convent girls were taken by force in broad daylight. The brigands had chosen those whose families could pay the highest ransom. By a lucky exception to the custom of bandits, the girls were treated with all the respect due to their sad situation. The ransom for each varied from two hundred to one thousand scudi.

Gasparoni, moreover, strictly observed all the out-ward forms of religion. His troop never committed a robbery or a murder on a Friday. On this day, and all others decreed by the Church, they faithfully fasted, and once a month they sent for a priest to confess them. Out of terror and all kinds of other reasons, no priest ever hesitated to absolve them.

A woman with whom Gasparoni had a liaison became the instrument used by the authorities to destroy this band and to capture Gasparoni along with some of his people. The Roman police lured the woman, who could not resist, with the bait of a reward of six thousand scudi. The brigand thus fell into a trap that she had laid. He came confidently into a wood where they had made an assignation, but soon realizing that his mistress had betrayed him he contrived to strangle her before being taken by the police. The unfortunate woman was therefore unable to enjoy the fruits of her treachery.

Rondino, a native of Piedmont, destined to enter the military police, had reached the rank of sergeant as a reward for his bravery and his detective work. Having completed his period of service, he went back to his birthplace, where he began his criminal career by stabbing to death an uncle who had unjustly stolen his savings and, to add insult to injury, had beaten him up.

Having taken this first step, Rondino withdrew to the mountains, where he embarked on a campaign against the police, who from time to time came looking for him. His exploits against them caused him to be looked on as a hero by the local peasantry, who harboured a deep hatred for the persecutors of the *carbonari*. Over a period of two or three years, Rondino killed or wounded about fifteen gendarmes.

Mischance had turned Rondino into a criminal who often changed his place of refuge, but he never moved further than seven or eight leagues from the village near Turin where he had been born. He never stole, and when his ammunition or supplies were exhausted, he would ask the first passer-by for a quarter of a scudo to buy powder, lead, and bread. If anyone tried to give him more, he refused it.

This honest brigand nursed a deep contempt for murderers and thieves. The fact of having been outlawed in his eyes excused the unusual profession he followed. Once he nobly thwarted a band who had told him of their plans to rob the coffers of a councillor from Turin, whose carriage held forty thousand francs. Rondino defended the man against this band and refused any reward.

About six months ago poor Rondino fell into the hands of the law in the following way. He was going to spend the night at the presbytery. As always, he asked for all the keys. But the priest kept one by which he was able to smuggle out someone to fetch the carabinieri. Woken by his dog, which was endowed with the keenest instincts, Rondino managed to climb up to the clock tower, where he barricaded himself in. When day broke, he exchanged volleys of shots with the carabinieri. He was unharmed, but several of his adversaries were put out of action. Lacking ammunition and supplies, he was forced to surrender. Rondino would only give himself up to the military, a detachment of which was entering the village at that very moment. Smashing the butt of his gun and giving his dog to the commanding officer, Rondino surrendered without resistance. He waited a long time for his trial, listened calmly, and submitted to execution without weakness or bluster.

Who could refuse pity, even concern, for such a man? Forced into a criminal career by a circumstance in which, as it seemed to him, he had only exercised his legitimate rights, the unfortunate fellow always held to his principles and to a certain loyalty that many so-called honest men often lack.

To end this sketch of the manners and customs of the extraordinary men who won their laurels on the highroads, here is the story of the notorious Barbone, who, according to some, is now a pensioner on day-release while to others he is the custodian of the Castel Sant'Angelo, where he has been imprisoned for some time.

Born in Velletri, Barbone was apprenticed to his heinous profession from his earliest years. His mother Rinalda was his teacher. He was the offspring of a liaison between this woman and a certain Peronti, who had gone from the altar to the forest. Having by some brilliant stroke obtained a lucrative reward from the government, together with an amnesty, this renegade priest eschewed brigandage and went back to preaching the word of God in his parish.

Barbone's mother, furious at being betrayed by a man whom she had loved passionately, thought of nothing but revenge. She did everything in her power to get her son to share the hatred she nourished, and only awaited the moment when he would be old enough to help her exact retribution. Rinalda wanted to burn the traitor at the foot of his own altar, but Peronti died a natural death, and Rinalda's despair at not being able to enjoy revenge hastened her demise.

Barbone did not lie about his origins. With a seasoned troop of fighters he became the terror of travellers, especially in the outskirts of Tivoli, Palestrina, and Poli. Having perpetrated every crime in the book, Barbone felt the need for a rest. Taking his example from Sulla, he tried to descend from the pinnacle of power. He made an offer to the pope to abandon his dictatorship on condition that he receive an indemnity and total absolution. The Holy Father accepted the offer. As proof of his sincerity, Barbone sent the pope the insignia of his position.

When this famous bandit made his entrance into the capital of the Christian world in 1818, crowds followed on his heels. The thought of being able to get close enough without danger to someone who had been the terror of the country had a certain allure. Besides, Rome always feels sympathy, even concern, for a murderer, who is often accorded the pity that should be given to his victim. How can we explain this strange emotion? It is a characteristic of these people. Place them between the murderer and the murdered, all that worries them is the danger that the former may be in. While watching a man who has committed the most atrocious crimes taken to prison, you will hear someone say, '*Poverino! Ha ammazzato un uomo!*' 'The poor fellow! He's killed a man', or, 'He was unlucky.'

The people have got used to seeing Barbone as he strolls along the streets of Rome. Nowadays, he is looked on without surprise but always admiringly. He walks about confidently with all the ease of a man whose conscience is clear.

To the names of the brigands who achieved deplorable celebrity should be added those of Stefano Spadolini; Pietro Mancino; Gobertinco, who, we are informed, killed nine hundred and seventy people and died regretting that he had not lived long enough to fulfil his vow to kill a thousand; Angelo del Duca; Oronzo Albegna, who killed his father, his mother, two brothers and a sister still in the cradle; Veneranda Porta and Stefano Fantini from Venice.

The existence of these bandits in Italy is, however, not an evil without remedy or an inconvenience inherent to certain areas. Men of character, who held the reins of the State at different times, were well able to suppress them.

Nicola Rienzi, who in 1347 became master of Rome and was granted the title of tribune, purged the country of brigands, by which it had been infested. Made a senator of Rome in 1354, this remarkable man had Fra Monreale executed. Having openly followed the profession of thief, the Fra died a hero. At the head of a free band, the first that desolated Italy, Monreale enriched himself and became a formidable presence. He had money in all the banks. In Padua alone he had sixty thousand ducats.

Sixtus V pursued the brigands relentlessly, allowing no one but himself to dispose of the lives and fortunes of his subjects. Outlaws who escaped punishment by flight and landless, lawless men, fled to neighbouring princes, who complained. Sixtus merely told them that all they had to do was to copy him or to hand their estates over to him. The bandits, thus tracked down, grew tired of their profession and disappeared.

One day, wanting to see the robbers from close up, Sixtus V disguised himself as a peasant and, taking to the road with a donkey laden with wine, he set off for the woods where outlaws had been seen. The bandits soon seized him, the donkey, and the wine. They put Sixtus to work turning a spit, while they ate, drank, and mocked him. But the crafty pope had put opium in the wine. The narcotic worked silently. Sixtus V waited for the right moment, gave a whistle, and his soldiers, hiding a short distance away, captured the whole band, who were sunk in a deep slumber.

Towards the end of the eighteenth century, a hundred years after the death of Sixtus V, the Marchese del Carpio, Naples' last viceroy, also successfully hunted down brigands. There were so many of them that to travel safely in this beautiful country people had to get together in convoys. Some bandits made treaties with the viceroy on condition of receiving an amnesty. The marchese had many of them put to death by the sword or by the executioner's hand; others he put to use on public works.

The three popes who succeeded Sixtus V did not seem to share his views on brigands. Either that or their reigns were too short for them to concern themselves with policing the highroads. Brigands therefore reappeared on the Church lands and – until Pius VII realized somewhat late his mistaken policy, and Leo XII managed to drive them almost entirely from the country during his reign – no pope suppressed them.

Under Napoleon the French contained these bands of assassins by wise and vigorous measures, and during their short period of administration Romans and the other Italian peoples enjoyed a security unknown for several centuries.

In 1814, when Pius VII was restored to power, the first thing he did was to grant an absolute pardon to a number of robber bands. The Rocagorga band was one of these. The pope's dispensation only increased the audacity of the brigands. Five years later he had to retract it by resorting to draconian measures. Cardinal Consalvi, taking the lead from what had been done for the town of Montefortino in 1557 under Paul IV, ordered the razing of Sonnino, a town which had become a rallying point and refuge for a large number of murderers. Nothing could have been more severe than Consalvi's edict of 18 July 1819. Anyone who gave food, money, or even shelter to a brigand did so on pain of death. No one was immune, not even the brigands' immediate families.

The right of sanctuary, often abolished, re-established, or modified, was one of the greatest encouragements to brigandage. A man who has committed a murder or robbed travellers on the highroads takes refuge in a cardinal's palace, or under the portico of a church, or in the compound of an embassy, or in a convent. There he lives safe and sound, cocking a snook at the agents of public order and ransoming passers-by when occasion presents itself. Bands of wretches of both sexes throng together in this way, living in a repulsive sort of commune, giving themselves over to the most sordid debauchery and fostering a hotbed for beggary. Murderers, fratricides, poisoners, arsonists, deserters, robbers, unfrocked monks, etc., etc., live cheek by jowl in the same sanctuary. They sneak out, commit further thefts or murders, and when pursued they rush back to the place that ensures their impunity.

As well as these refuges, many Roman bishops, princes, and lords' palaces enjoy privileges that prevent the police from entering without the owners' permission. In a third to half of the city, bandits can readily find refuge and shelter from any threat. It is easy to imagine how difficult it is to capture these criminals should the police by chance cast off their instinct for self-preservation and set out to hunt someone down.

Even in ancient Rome criminals enjoyed a right of sanctuary in pagan temples, and after AD 355 the same privilege was accorded to Christian churches.

One of the main sanctuaries in Rome was the great stairway of the Trinità dei Monti. The friends and families of decent men who had their homes in that quarter would bring in all the provisions they needed by day because by night the place was infested with malefactors. After a short while the crimes they committed would be forgotten and once again they would revert to their old ways.

These days robber bands have been dispersed and more or less eliminated. A few intrepid attacks still take place on the highways, but, all in all, with regard to murdering thieves, you can travel in Italy almost as safely as you can in France.

3

Preface to *The Cenci*
by Percy Bysshe Shelley

Shelley's five-act tragedy was written and first published in Italy, in 1819, when he was twenty-six years old. His intention was to have the play acted in Covent Garden, and towards this end he already had in mind the actress and actor he wished to play the main roles. But he was soon informed that the subject of incest – despite his delicate treatment of it – could not 'be admitted on the stage.' In fact, as his wife later wrote, 'in the course of the play, [Shelley] had never mentioned expressly Cenci's worst crime.' He even closed the drama short of the well-known and lurid executioner's block. All to no avail. It is interesting to note in the third sentence below Shelley's usage of the word 'mother-in-law' for 'stepmother', an early conflation that continued well into the nineteenth century. For a scrupulously documented account of the Cenci affair that offers a new reading of the historical facts (contradicting much of the romantic version of events that has come down to us from Stendhal, Shelley, and others), see Charles Nicholl's essay 'Screaming in the Castle', in the *London Review of Books*, 2 July 1998.

*

A manuscript was communicated to me during my travels in Italy, which was copied from the archives of the Cenci Palace at Rome, and contains a detailed account of the horrors which ended in the extinction of one of the noblest and richest families of that city during the Pontificate of Clement VIII, in the year 1599. The story is, that an old man having spent his life in debauchery and wickedness, conceived at length an implacable hatred towards his children; which showed itself towards one daughter under the form of an incestuous passion, aggravated by every circumstance of cruelty and violence. This daughter, after long and vain attempts to escape from what she considered a perpetual contamination both of body and mind, at length plotted with her mother-in-law and brother to murder their common tyrant. The young maiden, who was urged to this tremendous deed by an impulse which overpowered its horror, was evidently a most gentle and amiable being, a creature formed to adorn and be admired, and thus violently thwarted from her nature by the necessity of circumstance and opinion. The deed was quickly discovered, and, in spite of the most earnest prayers made to the Pope by the highest persons in Rome, the criminals were put to death. The old man had during his life repeatedly bought his pardon from the Pope for capital crimes of the most enormous and unspeakable kind, at the price of a hundred thousand crowns; the death therefore of his victims can scarcely be accounted for by the love of justice. The Pope, among other motives for severity, probably felt that whoever killed the Count Cenci deprived his treasury of a certain and copious source of revenue.* Such a story, if told so as to present to the reader all the feelings of those who once acted it, their hopes and fears, their confidences and misgivings, their various interests, passions, and opinions, acting upon and with each other, yet all conspiring to one tremendous end, would be as a light to make apparent some of the most dark and secret caverns of the human heart.

On my arrival at Rome I found that the story of the Cenci was a subject not to be mentioned in Italian society without awakening a deep and breathless interest; and that the feelings of the company never failed to incline to a romantic pity of the wrongs and a passionate exculpation of the horrible deed to which they urged her, who has been mingled two centuries with the common dust. All ranks of people knew the outlines of this history, and participated in the overwhelming interest which it seems to have the magic of exciting in the human heart. I had a copy of Guido's picture of Beatrice which is preserved

---

* The Papal Government formerly took the most extraordinary precautions against the publicity of facts which offer so tragical a demonstration of its own wickedness and weakness; so that the communication of the MS. had become, until very lately, a matter of some difficulty.

in the Colonna Palace, and my servant instantly recognized it as the portrait of *La Cenci*.

This national and universal interest which the story produces and has produced for two centuries and among all ranks of people in a great City, where the imagination is kept for ever active and awake, first suggested to me the conception of its fitness for a dramatic purpose. In fact it is a tragedy which has already received, from its capacity of awakening and sustaining the sympathy of men, approbation and success. Nothing remained as I imagined, but to clothe it to the apprehensions of my countrymen in such language and action as would bring it home to their hearts. The deepest and the sublimest tragic compositions, *King Lear* and the two plays in which the tale of Œdipus is told, were stories which already existed in tradition, as matters of popular belief and interest, before Shakespeare and Sophocles made them familiar to the sympathy of all succeeding generations of mankind.

This story of the Cenci is indeed eminently fearful and monstrous: anything like a dry exhibition of it on the stage would be insupportable. The person who would treat such a subject must increase the ideal, and diminish the actual horror of the events, so that the pleasure which arises from the poetry which exists in these tempestuous sufferings and crimes may mitigate the pain of the contemplation of the moral deformity from which they spring.

There must also be nothing attempted to make the exhibition subservient to what is vulgarly termed a moral purpose. The highest moral purpose aimed at in the highest species of the drama, is the teaching the human heart, through its sympathies and antipathies, the knowledge of itself; in proportion to the possession of which knowledge, every human being is wise, just, sincere, tolerant and kind. If dogmas can do more, it is well: but a drama is no fit place for the enforcement of them. Undoubtedly, no person can be truly dishonoured by the act of another; and the fit return to make to the most enormous injuries is kindness and forbearance, and a resolution to convert the injurer from his dark passions by peace and love. Revenge, retaliation, atonement, are pernicious mistakes. If Beatrice had thought in this manner she would have been wiser and better; but she would never have been a tragic character: the few whom such an exhibition would have interested, could never have been sufficiently interested for a dramatic purpose, from the want of finding sympathy in their interest among the mass who surround them. It is in the restless and anatomizing casuistry with which men seek the justification of Beatrice, yet feel that she has done what needs justification; it is in the superstitious horror with which they contemplate alike her wrongs and their revenge, that the dramatic character of what she did and suffered, consists.

I have endeavoured as nearly as possible to represent the characters as they probably were, and have sought to avoid the error of making them actuated by my own conceptions of right or wrong, false or true: thus under a thin veil converting names and actions of the sixteenth century into cold imperson-ations of my own mind. They are represented as Catholics, and as Catholics deeply tinged with reli-gion. To a Protestant apprehension there will appear something unnatural in the earnest and perpetual sentiment of the relations between God and men which pervade the tragedy of the Cenci. It will espe-cially be startled at the combination of an undoubting persuasion of the truth of the popular religion with a cool and determined perseverance in enormous guilt. But religion in Italy is not, as in Protestant countries, a cloak to be worn on particular days; or a passport which those who do not wish to be railed at carry with them to exhibit; or a gloomy passion for penetrating the impenetrable mysteries of our being, which terrifies its possessor at the darkness of the abyss to the brink of which it has conducted him. Religion coexists, as it were, in the mind of an Italian Catholic, with a faith in that of which all men have the most certain knowledge. It is interwoven with the whole fabric of life. It is adoration, faith, submis-sion, penitence, blind admiration; not a rule for moral conduct. It has no necessary connection with any one virtue. The most atrocious villain may be rigidly devout, and without any shock to established faith, confess himself to be so. Religion pervades intensely the whole frame of society, and is according to the temper of the mind which it inhabits, a passion, a persuasion, an excuse, a refuge; never a check. Cenci himself built a chapel in the court of his Palace, and dedicated it to St. Thomas the Apostle, and established masses for the peace of his soul. Thus in the first scene of the fourth act Lucretia's design in exposing herself to the consequences of an expostulation with Cenci after having administered the opiate, was to induce him by a feigned tale to confess himself before death; this being esteemed by Catholics as essential to salvation; and she only relinquishes her purpose when she perceives that her perseverance would expose Beatrice to new outrages.

I have avoided with great care in writing this play the introduction of what is commonly called mere poetry, and I imagine there will scarcely be found a detached simile or a single isolated description, unless Beatrice's description of the chasm appointed for her father's murder should be judged to be of that nature.*

In a dramatic composition the imagery and the passion should interpenetrate one another, the former being reserved simply for the full development and illustration of the latter. Imagination is as the immortal

* An idea in this speech was suggested by a most sublime passage in *El Purgatorio de San Patricio* of Calderon; the only plagiarism which I have intentionally committed in the whole piece.

God which should assume flesh for the redemption of mortal passion. It is thus that the most remote and the most familiar imagery may alike be fit for dramatic purposes when employed in the illustration of strong feeling, which raises what is low, and levels to the apprehension that which is lofty, casting over all the shadow of its own greatness. In other respects, I have written more carelessly; that is, without an over-fastidious and learned choice of words. In this respect I entirely agree with those modern critics who assert that in order to move men to true sympathy we must use the familiar language of men, and that our great ancestors the ancient English poets are the writers, a study of whom might incite us to do that for our own age which they have done for theirs. But it must be the real language of men in general and not that of any particular class to whose society the writer happens to belong. So much for what I have attempted; I need not be assured that success is a very different matter; particularly for one whose attention has but newly been awakened to the study of dramatic literature.

I endeavoured whilst at Rome to observe such monuments of this story as might be accessible to a stranger. The portrait of Beatrice at the Colonna Palace is admirable as a work of art: it was taken by Guido during her confinement in prison. But it is most interesting as a just representation of one of the loveliest specimens of the workmanship of Nature.

There is a fixed and pale composure upon the features: she seems sad and stricken down in spirit, yet the despair thus expressed is lightened by the patience of gentleness. Her head is bound with folds of white drapery from which the yellow strings of her golden hair escape, and fall about her neck. The moulding of her face is exquisitely delicate; the eyebrows are distinct and arched: the lips have that permanent meaning of imagination and sensibility which suffering has not repressed and which it seems as if death scarcely could extinguish. Her forehead is large and clear; her eyes, which we are told were remarkable for their vivacity, are swollen with weeping and lustreless, but beautifully tender and serene. In the whole mien there is a simplicity and dignity which, united with her exquisite loveliness and deep sorrow, are inexpressibly pathetic. Beatrice Cenci appears to have been one of those rare persons in whom energy and gentleness dwell together without destroying one another: her nature was simple and profound. The crimes and miseries in which she was an actor and a sufferer are as the mask and the mantle in which circumstances clothed her for her impersonation on the scene of the world.

The Cenci Palace is of great extent; and though in part modernized, there yet remains a vast and gloomy pile of feudal architecture in the same state as during the dreadful scenes which are the subject of this tragedy. The Palace is situated in an obscure corner of Rome, near the quarter of the Jews, and from the upper windows you see the immense ruins of Mount Palatine half hidden under their profuse overgrowth of trees. There is a court in one part of the Palace (perhaps that in which Cenci built the Chapel to St. Thomas), supported by granite columns and adorned with antique friezes of fine workmanship, and built up, according to the ancient Italian fashion, with balcony over balcony of open-work. One of the gates of the Palace formed of immense stones and leading through a passage, dark and lofty and opening into gloomy subterranean chambers, struck me particularly.

Of the Castle of Petrella, I could obtain no further information than that which is to be found in the manuscript.

4

On the Cenci Portrait
by Charles Dickens

'There is, probably not a famous Picture or Statue in all Italy, but could be easily buried under a mountain of printed paper devoted to dissertations on it. I do not, therefore, though an earnest admirer of Painting and Sculpture, expatiate at any length on famous Pictures and States.' So wrote Charles Dickens in the foreword to his *Pictures from Italy*, published in 1846, a book he characterized as 'a series of faint reflections . . . of places to which the imagination of most people are attracted in a greater or less degree, on which mine had dwelt for years. . . . The greater part of the descriptions were written on the spot, and sent home, from time to time, in private letters.' Here, from Chapter 10, is his reflection on Guido Reni's painting of Beatrice Cenci. It is significant that while he obviously knew and was attracted by the Cenci story he discreetly avoids any mention of it in his account of the picture.

The portrait of Beatrice di Cenci, in the Palazzo Berberini [sic], is a picture almost impossible to be forgotten. Through the transcendent sweetness and beauty of the face, there is a something shining out, that haunts me. I see it now, as I see this paper, or my pen. The head is loosely draped in white; the light hair falling down below the linen folds. She has turned suddenly towards you; and there is an expression in the eyes – although they are very tender and gentle – as if the wildness of a momentary terror, or distraction, had been struggled with and overcome, that instant; and nothing but a celestial hope, and a beautiful sorrow, and a desolate earthly helplessness remained. Some stories say that Guido painted it, the night before her execution; some other stories, that he painted it from memory, after having seen her, on her way to the scaffold. I am willing to believe that, as you see her on his canvas, so she turned towards him, in the crowd, from the first sight of the axe, and stamped upon his mind a look which he has stamped on mine as though I had stood beside him in the concourse. The guilty palace of the Cenci: blighting a whole quarter of the town, as it stands withering away by grains: had that face, to my fancy, in its dismal porch, and at its black, blind windows, and flitting up and down its dreary stairs, and growing out of the darkness of the ghostly galleries. The History is written in the Painting; written, in the dying girl's face, by Nature's own hand. And oh! how in that one touch she puts to flight (instead of making kin) the puny world that claims to be related to her, in right of poor conventional forgeries!

Glossary

Titles, terms of rank and/or office, hierarchies and distinctions, make frequent appearances in Stendhal. In the Roman tales, such titles are sometimes translated by the author into French and sometimes left in Italian or sometimes given in both. Dignities for the same office often varied among the several Italian republics, duchies, and principalities. Not all of the terms elaborated below figure in the Stendhal stories, but they do give colour and a pungent flavour of Italian style. The following list, compiled from Stendhal's pages and from Barbara Reynolds's *Cambridge Italian Dictionary*, should prove of interest.

bargello police constable, chief of secret police of Italian villages
bravi mercenaries, brigands
carbonari members of an early nineteeth-century secret society formed for the liberation and unification of Italy
cavaliere knight, member of a chivalric order, member of the nobility
condottiere mercenary, leader of a city's militia, soldier of fortune commanding troops

confortatore a prison chapel where the condemned
    receive the last ministrations of a priest

confortatori a society of men who accompany and
    offer consolation to the condemned

corte di Roma Roman Curia, the Papal Court, a
    royal court and not a court of law

donna A title used before Christian names; the wife
    or daughter of a prince, duke, marquis, count, or
    baron; in the south of Italy there is a wide courtesy
    use of '*Donna*', much like '*Signora*' elsewhere; also
    used of Benedictine nuns, corresponding to 'Dame'

Eccellenza title given to bishops

Eminenza title given to cardinals

illustrissimo old courtesy title (abbreviated '*Ill.mo*')

magistrato official entrusted with administration of
    the laws, local judiciary officer

magnate noble or important citizen

magnifico title bestowed on Venetian magnates,
    grandee

Monsignor Vescovo his lordship the Bishop

morra a game in which one player guesses the
    number of fingers held up by another

podestà administrative head of a town, mayor chosen
    by central government

principe signore ruling prince

rettore ruler, governor

sbirro police spy

scudiere squire, equerry, groom

signora lady, also a courtesy title

signoretto petty tyrant
signoria governing body of a medieval town council
signorone grand gentleman
signorotto country squire
Vostra Signoria Illustrissimo Your Lordship

STENDHAL, the favourite pen name of Marie-Henri Beyle, was the author of two of the world's greatest novels, *The Red and the Black* (1830) and *The Charterhouse of Parma* (1839). Born in Grenoble on 23 January 1783, he died in Paris on 23 March 1842. A prolific writer of autobiographical works, diaries, biographies, travel books, and novels – a number of them left unfinished – Stendhal was a great lover of Italian opera, La Scala, and Milan. He was part of Napoleon's army in the 1812 retreat from Moscow. In the 1830s he served as French consul at Civitavecchia, near Rome. While they commanded the acclaim of such notables as Balzac and Mérimée, Stendhal's writings – as he noted – were for the happy few. He enjoyed little success in his lifetime but predicted he would be widely read fifty years after his death. The claim was uncannily accurate.

SUSAN ASHE, who was born in northern India, moved to England in 1947. She has studied French at Grenoble, where Stendhal was born, and has produced literary translations from the French, Italian, and Spanish. She co-authored the much acclaimed English version of Esteban Echeverría's Argentine classic *The Slaughteryard*, published in 2010 in The Library of Lost Books. She has written three children's books, *Cuda of the Celts* (2003), *Fillet and the Mob* (2004), and *The Marmaduchess of Pontefract* (2011).

NORMAN THOMAS DI GIOVANNI has translated work by more than fifty Argentine writers, including ten volumes of stories and poems by Jorge Luis Borges. He is the author of *The Lesson of the Master*, a volume of essays on Borges and his work, which also appears in The Library of Lost Books along with his edition of *The Slaughteryard*. In 1991, the Argentine government appointed di Giovanni a Commander of the Order of May, their highest cultural honour.

Other Titles by Susan Ashe and Norman Thomas
di Giovanni in The Library of Lost Books

THE SLAUGHTERYARD

An amazing read. Beautifully translated. Everything in this
book is fascinating; the story itself, of course, but also the
glossary and the appendixes and the introduction. It is sad to
think, yet again, that men are the same little shits they've
always been. Mob violence. Mob rule, the idea of civility but
a distant dream, the notion of peace an even more distant
dream.

– Mark Strand

Norman Thomas di Giovanni and Susan Ashe have brought
this acute and desolate story into vivid English, beginning
with the title. Di Giovanni has also fleshed out the historical
background with apt quotations from the nineteenth century
so that the tale can be fully read today as story and history as
if the events narrated had just happened.

– Jason Wilson

If *The Slaughteryard* is the ur-text from which the literature of
Argentina flows, Peron, Peronism, the juntas, and the strongmen
who litter the history of the Argentine seem utterly predictable.
All the stuff in the appendixes is brilliant too. This is an excellent
book and deserves to be read widely.

– Carlo Gébler

The translation is excellent . . . but particularly useful are the glossary and the appendixes. *The Slaughteryard* is one of the most famous short stories in Spanish American literature, yet for decades people read around its most shocking detail, namely the intention of anal rape of a man by other men. The *mazorca* references are unequivocal. You have done us a great service by putting all this material in one book.

– Nicolas Shumway

For me, this translation is the lovechild of a beautiful affair with language. The narrative is truly seamless and it excited me in a way that other novels never will. *The Slaughteryard* is a powerful piece of writing. It is remarkable, is unforgettable. It really deserves to be read.

– Caroline Smailes

The Slaughteryard is a powerful and memorable tale, packed with information and colour, observation and, above all, political indictment. Translated with enormous vigour by erstwhile Borges collaborator and translator Norman Thomas di Giovanni and Susan Ashe, it provides an insight into a world that's both recognisably modern and tantalisingly 'other', which is just what you expect from a classic 'lost book'. It's packed with gems. The book not only introduces and contextualises one of South America's greatest stories but also delights on its own terms. I recommend it.

– Charles Lambert

Fortunately . . . di Giovanni has supplied a substantial introduction and glossary which do an excellent job of providing context . . . The result is a powerful piece of work. The presentation of *The Slaughteryard* in this volume is an excellent example of how to make an old text accessible to contemporary general readers whilst still allowing them to discover that text for themselves.

– David Hebblethwaite

THE LESSON OF THE MASTER

In *The Lesson of the Master*, di Giovanni tells the story of his literary adventures with Borges. The book is an engaging mix of memoir, scholarship and criticism, indispensable to the Borges buff; it is also an excellent lesson in the art of writing.

– Kaiser Haq

A personal memoir describing the author's close friendship with Borges in Buenos Aires in the last years of the great man's life prefaces a collection of di Giovanni's critical essays that rely for their authority largely on the word of Borges himself, supplemented by some detective work by di Giovanni. Some Borges aficionados are irritated (to put it mildly) that di Giovanni's association with Borges quickly developed from the role of passive translator to active collaborator.

– *The Times*

The Lesson of the Master is a collection of essays and articles in which di Giovanni reveals the man behind the genius. It is less a biography of Borges . . . than a discussion about translation. Di Giovanni gives examples of the often comical way in which Borges has been badly translated. In one poem a translator came up with horses wearing helmets whilst Borges was talking about their hooves. At least Borges can be assured there is one translator whose fascinating and almost maniacal attention to detail will never allow for bad translation or the pursuit of a phony subtext.

– Edward Ashe

. . . this delightful little book of essays from which both translators in general and Borges's admirers in particular may profit a lot.

– Inés Pardal

. . . between 1967 and 1972, in collaboration with di Giovanni, Borges – blind, old and fearful of his powers fading – reworked some of his best stories and poems into what are arguably not just fine translations of the greatest Spanish language writer of the twentieth century, but some of twentieth-century English literature's finest original works. To his credit, di Giovanni makes no claim for himself other than his friendship and work with Borges, and his book is, by its own admission, a modest volume that seeks to be – and succeeds – an act of homage to Borges . . . These essays reveal Borges as a very human figure, an idea of the writer at odds with the monstrous literary genius he is too often lauded as being. Together they sought to honour Borges's glorious vision of what was possible with translation: work as good as, even better, than the original. To translate, for Borges, was an invitation to create no less significant than the invitation to write. Paradoxically, though their grail was not style, their 're-creations' contain English of beauty and some times dazzling virtuosity.

– Richard Flanagan

Readers of Jorge Luis Borges in English have good reason to be grateful to Norman Thomas di Giovanni. In collaboration with the author, he translated a series of the later books almost as they were written . . . He prompted Borges to compose a valuable memoir. He was also the instigator, organizer and editor of the wonderful *Selected Poems 1923-1967* . . . *The Lesson of the Master* looks back on the years of di Giovanni's close collaboration with Borges (1968 to 1972) and sketches a portrait of the artist as a frail and lonely old man, unhappily married and worried that he is finished as a writer. It also gives us precious glimpses of Borges at work . . .

– Chris Andrews

In these pages, Norman Thomas di Giovanni . . . tells the story that brought [Borges and him] together in their common passion – literature. By means of hitherto unknown anecdotes and subtle observations, di Giovanni shows and reads Borges in a way never before seen . . . Among all the book's themes, the mystery of translation occupies a central place, even to the point of putting forward a theory of translation.

– Soles

The Lesson of the Master amplifies and contradicts a good deal of the information of other biographies, such as those of María Esther Vázquez and Alicia Jurado, and offers in plain language and without the pretentiousness of many other studies, a lucid analysis of certain areas of Borges's work . . .

– Daniel Dessein

In these essays, Norman Thomas di Giovanni recounts his years in Buenos Aires and his view of the everyday life of the *porteños* of that era from a none-too-pious standpoint. The book is spiced with colourful anecdotes concerning the vicissitudes of the translator's craft.

– *La Nación Revista*